SOME FRIENDSHIPS NEVER DIE

Book Five

MONSTERS AND MAYHEM

E A COMISKEY

TRADEMARK ACKNOWLEDGEMENT

Piggly Wiggly
Titanic
Jeep Cherokee
Lego
Rice Krispies
Enterprise
Cadillac Coupe Deville
Velcro
Hobbits
Rivendell
Yoda
Cracker Barrel
Paul Harvey's The Rest of the Story
Star Wars
Jehovah's Witness
Prevost
Styrofoam
Tylenol
Bic
Centers for Disease Control (CDC)

Elvis Presley
Smith and Wesson
Sig Sauer
Oak Ridge Boys
Toyota
Ford Explorer
Reader's Digest
Chevy Trailblazer
Muhammed Ali
Holiday Inn Express
Jeep
Disney World
Humvee
Dollar Tree

CHAPTER ONE

Richard

THE FIRE-ENGINE-RED 1959 CADILLAC COUPE DEVILLE streaked across the jagged spine of the Rocky Mountains. On the vehicle's fine stereo, Elvis Presley sang about hound dogs. Bright winter sun beat down through the windshield, warming Richard Bell. In such grand moments, he could almost forget that the world was infested with blood-thirsty monsters. Each mile brought him and his companions closer to their next encounter, but just then, all was right with the world.

He took a bite of the burger he'd ordered from a roadside stand. Ketchup and bacon grease dripped down his chin. He closed his eyes and relished the savory mix of meat, onions, veggies, and cheese. In all his years of retirement and his brief stay at the old folks' home, he'd eaten only to stay alive. What a mistake! Eating wasn't a means to an end. Good food was, all by itself, a reason for living.

A salty French fry was the perfect complement to the

burger. He washed the food down with icy cold soda and was rewarded with a satisfying belch.

No one reproached him. *Weird.*

He peeked over his shoulder into the backseat. His grand-daughter—a woman old enough to have grandkids of her own, had she started at an early age—was canoodling with her new man-friend, Gordon Westchester. The two looked like teenagers, whispering and giggling with their heads together. They'd been that way since they left Santa Fe a day and a half earlier.

Stanley Kapcheck sat in the driver's seat, dapper in his zippered sweater and blue jeans. He wore a pair of over-priced sunglasses and a newsboy cap that covered his shiny bald head. Richard thought he looked like a wrinkled old raisin striving too hard for a younger man's style, but judging by the way both women and men threw themselves at the geezer, he was doing something right. Richard gave a mental shrug. He'd rather be comfortable in his Hanes T-shirts. Besides, trading in the perfectly serviceable Wellington Plastics jacket he'd been wearing for the last twenty years seemed wasteful. Nothing wrong with it. Why buy new?

"You're pretty quiet," Richard said before taking another bite of the divine hamburger.

Stanley's thin lips twitched in a semblance of a smile. "I suppose the dialogue in my mind occupies me to the point of distraction."

"Voices in your head, eh? Always knew there was something wrong with you."

"Don't you converse with yourself in your thoughts?"

"I ain't crazy." Richard refused to get drawn into Stanley's nonsense. Talking to voices inside your own head—that's the kind of thing that got a man locked up in a padded room.

"My friend, we are old men chasing after death in an old car, armed with swords and wooden stakes. We're both certifiably insane."

Richard harrumphed. "You ain't got to say it that way. We're doing a service for this world."

"Yes. I suppose we are."

From the back seat, Burke chimed in. "Grandpa's right and Busar was doing a service, too. How many lives did he save? How many have you saved because of what he taught you?"

Stanley downshifted as they began a long, curving descent.

"Then you taught us, me and Burke, and now Gordon," Richard said. "We ain't even been doing this for a whole year yet, and we helped a heap of folks. It's good work, and it all started with Busar."

"It all started thousands of years before Busar was born," Stanley said. "He had a mentor, too, of course, just as he mentored me." With skillful ease, born from having driven thousands upon thousands of miles in his lifetime, Stanley maneuvered the car along a narrow stretch bordered by a solid rock wall on one side and a two-hundred-foot drop on the other. "Busar, as I knew him, is dead. My mentor was murdered in a horrible accident while we were hunting a monster that preyed on children. An honorable way to go, and that's how I prefer to think of it."

Richard scratched his head. He tried to pat down his white cloud of hair, realized he failed, and wondered why, after so many years, he kept trying. An idea nagged him since they left for this hunt, and he hadn't had the backbone to spit it out. It was now or never.

"We saved you, Stanley. Burke, too."

Nothing about Stanley's expression changed. As usual, he remained cool as a cucumber.

How annoying. It ain't natural.

Tension buzzed in the car like a fat, bloodthirsty mosquito.

In an attempt to swat it away, Richard barreled on with his theory. In for a penny, in for a pound. "You told us that Busar was fighting the monster, and his soul ripped, but you ripped too. Back when we fought on the beach in Michigan, they ripped part of you away, and that leprechaun fixed you up again." He took a sip of his soda to wash away the absurdity of that sentence. Talk about sending a guy to the loony bin! A year ago, he'd have thought such a comment the height of insanity, but he'd had his eyes opened since then. "Burke got split up, too."

A rustling of fabric from the back seat, then Burke appeared, leaning over the back of the seat. "I was never split. I was possessed."

"What's the difference?" Richard hated nitpicking.

"If something's split, it's only half. I was double. Still, I think you have a valid point. I've been wondering the same thing. There are all kinds of cures for—"

"There is no cure." Stanley's flat tone left no room for argument, but he'd softened back to his usual over-dandied style when he spoke again. "Forgive me, my dear. I don't mean to be churlish, but my spirit is weary, and I cannot bear the discussion of miracles when the likelihood is so slim."

Burke squeezed Stanley's arm and scooted back next to Gordon again.

"Okay, so I'm the new guy," Gordon growled, his voice like crushed lava stone. "I've seen enough that I get the general idea. I met the sea god and fought a monster on the cruise ship. I saw what happened back there in Santa Fe when Burke's ex played with magic. Consider my mind opened, but I'd like a little more in-depth explanation of what we're heading into here. What are you thinking we're going to do when we get there?"

The same questions occurred to Richard repeatedly, but he'd been too big of a chicken to put them out there like that.

He wasn't entirely sure he wanted to know the answers. Sometimes ignorance was bliss.

White wall tires hummed a tenor melody over the V8 engine's bass growl. The three less-experienced hunters waited for Stanley to teach them something new.

"Certain creatures cross cultural boundaries. Every culture, no matter how primitive or modern, share the ancient stories of demons, blood drinkers, vengeful spirits, and so on and so forth. The monsters of the legends that spread across the globe are the most ancient and most powerful."

Richard still had a third of a cheeseburger lying on a wrapper on his lap. Cooler now, it was a bit past his peak, but still infinitely better than the olive loaf sandwiches he'd lived off of for half a century before Stanley sprung him out of the old folk's home.

Stanley slowed behind a semi, peeked around at the oncoming traffic, and passed as smooth as a seasoned racecar driver. "Busar was killed fighting an entity so old its name has been lost to antiquity."

Once again, the urge to point out that Busar wasn't dead rose up in Richard like a burp, but he managed to force it back down. He would have said it a year ago. He was growing as a person.

"So, you're saying that the old things are the worst, and this one is the oldest of all?" Gordon asked.

"Not the oldest of all, I should think, but old beyond human memory. For lack of a better term, we're about to pick a fight with the boogeyman," Richard said.

Now that the burger was gone, Richard wondered if the entire meal might have been poor judgment. It sat in his gut like a brick. He took another drink of soda, hoping to work himself up to a proper belch to relieve the pressure. Admitting that it was fear churning in his protruding belly was out of the question. Almost certainly, it was the greasy food.

"My mama told me the boogeyman was a figment of my imagination," Gordon said.

Stanley's gaze never left the road. "Your mother also told you all souls went to Heaven. She was mistaken."

Once again, Burke's head popped up between them. Kid used to be some kind of a hippie-dippie yoga master, always breathing deep and finding her Zen. Give her a few days with a deep-voiced ex-soldier and, all of a sudden, she's restless as a worm in hot ashes.

"You've been talking around the edges of this hunt since the subject of Busar came up back in Santa Fe. Spell it out. What are we heading into? Let's make a plan. It'll be better for you than letting your thoughts eat you from the inside out," she said.

They reached a more level stretch of pavement, and Stanley adjusted the gearshift. "Your wisdom exceeds your years."

"I have plenty of years," Burke said.

Gordon whispered something Richard couldn't make out, and Burke flashed a grin in his direction.

Good lord. Maybe his indigestion wasn't caused by the food after all. Still, the kid had a point. "We got nothing but time. There's what? Another six hundred miles between here and there?"

Stanley's nod was so subtle it might have been a twitch of his old muscles if only Stanley's old muscles ever twitched. No man who remembered the Roaring Twenties had a right to be steady as steel. Time is a transaction. For every day living, a body has to give up a piece of itself. So far as he could tell, the only thing Stan Kapcheck ever had to give up was his hair.

"Are you okay?" Burke asked.

Richard twisted around to look at her. "Me? I'm fine. Why?"

"You had a look on your face like you just ate a sour pickle. You're not car sick, are you? These twisty roads—"

"I'm fine," Richard groused. "Can we stick to the subject, please? Spill it, Stan. You've got to do it sooner or later."

"I'll begin with the monster, and perhaps that will help you understand about Busar. As I said, we're fighting the boogeyman. It's an entity that, like a ghost, can be there one moment and gone the next, but trapping it is far more difficult than trapping a ghost or even a demon. No mere salt line or devil's trap will hold it."

"But it can be trapped?" Burke asked.

"It can, but it's powerful magic that requires tools beyond what we have."

"A hunter is led to the hunt. The tools tend to be there when we need them." Burke was parroting something Stanley had repeated a thousand times.

"Yes, but...." Stanley let that argument drift away and started on a different track. "Children have an uncanny sense of this creature's presence. It terrifies them, and it feeds on their terror. It will play with them, sometimes for months, even years, before it destroys them. The deaths themselves will seem so natural no one ever thinks to question. A little one will develop a fever, they'll be lethargic. The child's condition deteriorates from that point."

"It could be the flu, so far as everyone around them is concerned," Burke observed.

"And so hunters rarely become aware," Stanley added.

Gordon piped up from the back seat. "Even if they're aware, what can they do against something that can't be killed and is nearly impossible to trap?"

"You've come to the crux of the problem," Stanley said.

Richard remembered something that had been mentioned when all this first came up. "You told us before that Busar had a talisman he was using."

"He did."

"Can we get something like that again?"

"Something like a magical seven-thousand-year-old artifact?" Stanley shrugged a bony shoulder. "So far as I know, the one we had was the only one that existed, but I'm open to suggestions if you know where such a thing might be found."

"You have connections," Richard pointed out.

"Having connections doesn't make the acquisition of such objects as simple as popping into the local Piggly Wiggly, Dick."

Richard harrumphed. Lord, but he hated being called Dick, and Stan Kapcheck darn well knew it.

"Even if we had such an object," Stanley went on, "the risk is too high. I won't watch what happened to Busar happen to any of you. I won't make this journey a second time."

"Maybe The Children of Cain could help us," Burke suggested.

Now *that* was a humdinger of an idea. No one had more powerful objects than the super-secret organization that governed the world's monsters.

"My dear, don't forget that The Children of Cain are on the side of the monsters, not the humans. The only reason they helped us in the past is because it suited their needs at that moment. I will remind you, as well, that a part of their kindness toward us had to do with The Devil's hands-off order. I suspect after recent events she may not be so inclined to offer me her protection."

Oh, yeah. The Devil probably wanted to kill them. That was a problem. Richard opened the glovebox and fished out a bottle of antacids.

"Do I want to know who The Children of Cain are?" Gordon asked.

"No," the three others said in unison.

"Is this boogeyman mentioned in the books of lore?" Burke asked.

"Of course," Stanley said.

"You going to tell us what it says, or are we playing twenty questions to pass the time?" Richard asked.

"The lore says the creatures are to be avoided at all costs." Stanley's plumb line posture drooped a little. "You're all failing to see the main point." He sighed and sat up straight again as if steeling himself. "The creature Busar and I fought died when Busar did."

Richard opened his mouth to argue about Busar being dead, but Stanley held up a hand to silence him.

"Children were dying. When Busar.... When all that happened, the deaths stopped. I don't know where Busar went, but the deaths stopped, and the child we were helping thrived and grew up. I kept tabs on her and on the area all this time. I don't know where Busar went, but the deaths stopped."

"And now it's started again," Burke said.

Stanley nodded. "Yes. Two children have passed away in the last year, both from a mysterious, undiagnosed illness, but the monster is dead. The odds of another coming to the same place are hard to put stock in. Boogymen are fiercely territorial, and only a few of the creatures exist."

The edge of the setting sun dipped behind the mountain, casting the landscape into sudden twilight. Stanley removed his sunglasses and stowed them in the center console. His gaze met Burke's in the rearview mirror. "I told you before. A human with half a soul is neither in this world nor the next. He cannot live, cannot experience pleasure, cannot love, cannot exist among whole humans without causing constant violent disruption to the balance of their lives, whether that's what he desires or not. Nor can he die, as a significant piece of him is already crossed over. He is trapped in his existence, living in an unending battle of what he was and what he cannot become."

"I can't quite wrap my mind around what you're telling us," Gordon growled. "I get the idea, but I guess I haven't seen enough of this kind of thing to accept it the way you all do.

That said, maybe my question is ignorant. If that's the case, I thank you for helping me get up to speed. If Busar successfully eliminated the monster and you say another of the same kind is unlikely to hunt in the same area, then we're not hunting this so-called boogeyman. And you said yourself that you've kept an eye on the area. If Busar had turned serial killer or some such thing, you'd have known long before now. It's not Busar hurting these children. He doesn't have the power to drain them like the other creature does."

"Maybe they're just getting sick," Burke suggested.

"Maybe Busar started walking north and ended up hunting whales in the arctic sea," Richard said.

"Maybe there's a different monster causing this trouble. Are there other monsters on the Olympic Peninsula?" Gordon asked.

"My friend, there are so many monsters on the Olympic Peninsula that our first challenge will be figuring out who the humans are," Stanley replied.

A low burp finally worked its way out of Richard, providing a small measure of relief. "So, what you're telling us is that there might be an unkillable monster hurting little kids. It could be Busar, or maybe not. No one knows for sure, and he's unkillable, too. Meanwhile, in order to get to the two immortals, we've got to navigate a rainforest full of spooks during a time when the leaders of the spooks might just have it out for us because you had a messy breakup with your girlfriend, The Devil. Assuming she's reassembled herself from the pile of ash you left her in, she might also be coming after us at any moment."

For the first time since they left the restaurant, Stanley reached for the cup of tea he'd ordered and took a long drink. After he set it back in the cup holder, he nodded. "I think you're starting to get the idea."

Burke retreated to her place next to Gordon.

"So, we're about as screwed as a port hooker the day after the navy docks," Richard muttered.

"Yes, about that screwed," Stanley agreed. He sipped his tea again. The little lines around his eyes scrunched like crepe paper as a smile crossed his face. "I'm glad you're all with me. I take great comfort in your presence."

Richard had been dying alone in a nursing home when Stanley found him. As far as he could figure, every day since then had been borrowed time, so what the heck. If a man had to go, he might as well go down in a blaze of glory. Thinking of it that way, Richard had to admit that he took great comfort in being part of their little posse, too. Still, they'd be having a snowball fight in Hell before he admitted it out loud to Stanley freaking Kapcheck.

CHAPTER TWO

Ben

BEN LOCKED HIS BEDROOM DOOR. WITH HIS FOOT, HE shoved the little braided rug up against the crack at the bottom and stuffed a tissue into the keyhole before propping a chair under the knob to ensure no one entered. His mother wasn't the type to barge in without knocking, but what if today was the day? What if some guest came, and she told them to use the upstairs bathroom, and they picked the wrong door? If the police showed up and....

He snickered. It was too absurd of a notion to entertain. There was no way anyone could trace a thing back to him. His hands were clean. No trail existed—he was certain of that.

Still, extreme care was only prudent.

To that end, he tugged the string that closed the heather gray blinds over the room's single window.

As often happened in the moments preceding decisive action, doubt pricked his heart. What if it didn't work? Maybe he was going about this all wrong. Had he misjudged the character of the players in the game?

"You're too smart for that," he assured himself.

Possibly, the unusual heat in the closet doorknob was just his imagination. Perhaps the buzz of power inside that small sanctuary existed only in his mind. Or the power within him had grown to such immensity a single human vessel could not contain it any longer. It had seeped out of his pores and infiltrated the sacred space where he performed his holy labor of love.

He found the box of matches on the shelf and rasped one across the abrasive strip. Fire flickered to life and illuminated his sanctuary. The touch of match to wick lit two pillar candles, shook the match out, and pulled the door shut, sealing away the world and its myriad distractions. He knelt before the altar.

In front of the left candle was a small bowl of water. A small bowl of earth sat before the other. He lit a stick of incense and placed it in the holder directly in front of him. It symbolized air. The perfect balance of the space lent him a feeling of peace he'd never known anywhere else. He knelt, sat back on his heels, and sighed with contentment.

Now is not the time for relaxing, he chided himself.

Indeed, there was work to be done, so he slid the wooden box where he kept his treasures from its storage place and lifted the lid. On top of the little collection was a photograph of Stanley Kapcheck leaning against his treasured red convertible, grinning as if he hadn't a care in the world. The picture taunted Ben. The old photograph, taken when color prints were the latest technology, had faded to yellows and reds. Back then, the hunter was living on borrowed time. He had no business still walking the earth now, so many years later.

He'll die when they all die. He is not immortal.

Like a sprout bursting through the fertile soil of a sun-warmed garden in spring, glee found good ground in his heart and bloomed to life. Stanley Kapcheck would die. They would all die, and those who could not die would beg for that mercy.

After shifting the photograph to the bottom of the pile of odds and ends, he withdrew the folded paper with the list of names. Relatively speaking, it wasn't a very long list. Already, a few had been crossed off. He'd have to add more if this all drew on much longer. Hopefully, it wouldn't come to that.

This day you have your daily bread, a voice whispered in his mind.

Truth. No good would come from dwelling on maybes and what-ifs. For now, everything he needed was close at hand. It had all been promised, and it had all been provided. If he needed more at some future date, no doubt it would come to him, just like the rest.

With the fancy gold-and-black fountain pen his mother had given him last Christmas, he crossed off the first two names and turned his attention to the third.

This part was always difficult, but no good ever came without self-sacrifice.

He memorized the spelling of the third name, folded the sheet on its well-worn creases, tucked it back into the box, and returned to its place. A new sheet of paper, gleaming so brightly white it seemed to glow in the firelight, was waiting in the center of the altar. He set his athame atop the paper and took a deep breath before beginning the spell.

Chanting was an art as much as a science. He'd read about how to do it, but it took a lot of practice to make it effective. An expert now, he let the words fall from his lips, let the vibration of the sounds mesmerize him, felt the magic fill his veins and take over his mind. When he lifted the dagger, the magic left no room for fear. When he cut his arm, enchantment allowed no pain. Painting the name in blood was as automatic as leaving a signature on a receipt.

None of that mattered. The real battle happened in the place where the physical world ended, and the spiritual world began. A heavy curtain drew open. On one side stood Ben. On the other side, was Legion. To draw from their power, he had no choice but to let them in, but he must not give himself over, or they would devour him, leaving no more than a shell they could inhabit.

He would not allow himself to be used in that way. He was the master, and they would remain at his beck and call, but the will required to maintain that hierarchy crushed something within him. It was like breathing at the bottom of the ocean or standing beneath a mountain.

Unable to maintain the chant, he gritted his teeth together, and trembling with the effort, he drew the curtain shut and returned to himself. Sweat dripped into his eyes, drawing tears. Through the blur, he read the name written in his own blood but in handwriting utterly different from his, and he grinned with satisfaction.

The owner of the name would have to die a little sooner than the rest, but then Stanley would come; he would fulfill his duties, and his final duty would be to return to ashes and dust. He'd been a foolish child to doubt. Everything was proceeding just as it should. The plan was perfect.

CHAPTER THREE

Burke

DARKNESS DESCENDED WITH STARTLING SPEED IN THE mountains, and without the bright sunlight, the convertible cooled. Burke snuggled up against Gordon, taking pleasure in his warmth. He wrapped strong arms around her, and she welcomed them. For years, she'd defined herself by her husband's concept of her. After he left, she did everything she could to make herself so desirable he'd come back. It took a long time, far longer than she cared to admit, for her to reach a place where she could be comfortable in her skin as a single woman. Gordon had never been part of the plan.

Then again, hunting monsters with her grandfather and his geriatric best frenemy wasn't part of the plan either. Yet here she was. She wouldn't trade it for all the world.

"Are you scared?" A mere breath against her ear, Gordon's question raised goosebumps along her arms.

"No." And that was the truth. She felt safe and secure, and content.

He nuzzled in closer. "Are you the kind of soldier who's only scared when the rockets start launching?"

"I don't think so." That was true, too. She'd fought more battles than she could remember, but to the best of her recollection, she'd never frozen in terror. "Afterward, though."

"Yeah. That's when you have time to think about what might have happened, what you could have lost, all the things that might have gone wrong."

One of the things she loved most about him was his understanding and quiet acceptance of who she was.

In the front seat, her grandfather snored himself awake, shifted position, and immediately fell asleep again.

"You're sure Stan's okay to be driving? He's been at it for more than twelve hours straight."

"He's fine. He'll say something if he gets tired. He's got a lot on his mind."

Gordon's low, sexy laugh rumbled beneath her backbone. "You think?" His fingers laced together with hers. "I never met anybody like Stan. He's something."

"You don't know the half of it."

"I know The Devil Herself fell in love with him, and I think I get it. If I wasn't straight, I'd be smitten myself."

"Sounds like you have a bit of a crush anyway."

"It's what the kids these days are calling a bromance." A mile or so passed in contented silence before Gordon spoke again. "I'm afraid," he confessed.

"Of the boogeyman?" It sounded funny; no denying it.

"Well, yeah, that, but it's more than that. What if I'm the weak link? The one that gets someone killed?"

Burke wanted to say something about his Special Forces training, his years of being in charge of the security of thousands of travelers on the cruise ship, or even his strong body and lightning quick reflexes. Instead, she shifted to look into his eyes and said, "Gordon, my grandfather is an eighty-year-old retired plastics worker with a bad hip, and he's saved our butts more times than I can count. Stanley's right. If you're led to a hunt, you're given what you need to finish it."

"Except you told me that the only way out for a hunter is to die in a hunt. Clearly, they don't all have what they need to finish it."

From the front seat, Stanley proved that he was awake and paying attention. "Don't worry, my friend. They almost always die on the first hunt or after they've been around long enough to get cocky. You've already had your first, and you're still too green to overestimate yourself."

"You really know how to make a guy feel better," Gordon said.

The smile on Stanley's face was audible in his voice. "Well, I try." He gestured at a blue sign on the side of the road. "I'm going to pull off there. I thought we could stretch our legs. Do one of you want to drive for a while?"

Burke volunteered to take over.

EVERY NIGHT, UNOBSERVED BY MOST OF THE WORLD'S TWO-legged occupants, a deathlike stillness settles over the land like a velvety blanket. After the late-night revelers have been sent home to recover until five p.m. rolls around again, before the earliest risers have yet to hit snooze on their alarm for the first time of the morning, the earth holds its breath, and the monsters prowl.

Burke met that single hour of the night with dread and fascination. At no other time of day did she feel so alive, so connected with the primal roots that ran back to a distant ancestral matriarch hiding behind a fire at the mouth of a cave, listening to the sounds of prowling sabretooths on the other side of the light. At no other time did fear stalk her in the same eerie, intimate way.

During the witching hour, Death Himself might be the man she bumps into at the all-night gas station. And she wasn't speaking metaphorically about a thug with a handgun looking to score a few hundred bucks out of the cash register so he could use it for his next high. According to Stanley, Death was a real guy.

As far as she last heard, though, he lived in New York. The thought comforted her as she took a wide right turn into a well-lit truck stop on the Utah-Idaho border. The Cadillac slid onto the parking lot's asphalt with the gracefulness of a long-limbed dancer. Thanks to near-obsessive love and care, sixty-plus years of hard miles barely showed on the extraordinary vehicle. Burke knew her grandfather was half in love with the car, and she couldn't blame him. Hands down, it was the coolest thing she'd ever driven—far superior to the dime-a-dozen sedans Detroit had turned out in recent years.

The abrupt silencing of the engine caused Gordon and Stanley to stir in the back seat. Burke reached over and gave her grandfather a gentle shake. "Gas station. You need to go inside?"

Richard sat up straight with a groan and wiped the drool from the corner of his mouth. His hair on the right side stood up like a turkey's tail.

Chilly air blasted into the car's warm interior when Burke pushed the door open. It felt good to put her feet on solid ground and stretch to her full height. Someone walking across bubble wrap couldn't have created more popping noises than her spine made. She slipped a credit card from her back pocket and swiped it through the reader on the pump, set the handle to fill the tank.

Someone's watching me.

Casually, she reached both hands behind her back to stretch her shoulders and twisted her torso from side to side to work the kinks out. The motion gave her a one-hundred-eighty-degree view of the surrounding area. The gas station glowed like some alien crystal dropped into the unoccupied landscape. Two eighteen-wheelers rumbled near the diesel pumps on the other side of the lot. A single Chevy Trailblazer was parked in the angled spots near the building. A kid, maybe nineteen years old, wearing a blue vest with the station's logo on the breast, stood framed in the glass door. His body had the lanky look boys sometimes got when they grew tall faster than they could fill out the space offered. He wore his dark hair shaved close to his head.

One by one, the three men piled out of the car, each repeating some version of her stretching routine. Stanley stood next to her. Her grandfather and Gordon were on the other side.

Burke squatted down near the rear tire as if to inspect it. "Something's hinky, Stanley."

Stanley bounced on his toes, just a spry older man, getting the blood moving again. "I say, Richard, doesn't this station remind you of the truck stop where that redhead worked. You know the one in East Texas?"

"East Texas? You mean the one with the...oh. Does it?" Richard's shuffling step moved a few steps further away. "I'm not sure, but if you say so."

"Will you help me with this, Gordon?" Burke asked.

Wonderful Gordon—a man with a thousand questions and the good sense to wait for a better time to ask them—came around the back end of the car just as Stanley strolled off in the opposite direction.

"Your grandfather and I are going to use the restroom," Stanley said.

"You're armed?" she whispered. Burke stood up and leaned her back against the back door. In this direction, Death's dark kingdom stretched as far as the eye could see, marred by only a few inadequate streetlights and a single lamp attached to a post in some farmer's yard a mile away.

"Of course. What's wrong?"

"I don't know. Something." Every internal alarm she'd calibrated to near perfection in the past months flashed and buzzed.

The gas pump clicked off, and Gordon set it back in the cradle.

Burke leaned in to pull the keys from the ignition, walked around to the trunk, and popped it open. Four large duffle bags sat atop the false bottom that hid their treasure trove of weapons.

"You remember?" she asked.

"More or less. Iron for ghosts and fairies. Silver for shifters."

Richard and Stanley reached the building, but before they could open the door, the skinny kid pushed it open and stepped outside.

"Two o'clock," Gordon warned.

Burke looked as an older man, big as a tank with more hair than a grizzly, came around the corner. Dark red stains covered the front of the Grateful Dead tee shirt. She muttered a curse and drew the blade she kept holstered at her ankle. Steel, honed to a razor-edge, had no magical properties, but it would slow any creature with a physical form.

"I know who you are," the kid said.

Stanley slipped his hands into his pockets. "Have we met?"

The kid spat on the ground. "You killed my brother and his whole nest in California." His attention turned to the hairy tank. "Two old guys and a chick in an old Caddy."

Mr. Hairy stopped in his tracks and growled like the bear he resembled.

Muttering a curse, Burke yanked on the hidden handle of the false bottom and grabbed two stakes. "Vampires."

"Obviously," Gordon muttered, and took two stakes for himself from the full canvas bag they kept at the ready.

Hairy's attention turned toward them. "Stay there," he called out. "Take one step in this direction, and we'll rip the old guys' heads off right here in front of you."

"Why should she listen to you?" Stanley asked. "You do intend to rip our heads off, anyway, do you not?"

Skinny laughed—a high-pitched giggle better suited to a fourteen-year-old cheerleader than a strapping young monster. "For what you did, we're going to make you hurt, old man, but we'll drag you around back first, just in case any other idiots are out on this god-forsaken road. That'll give you at least two or three minutes to beg for mercy and pray to your pathetic excuse of a god to save you." He advanced toward Stanley.

Richard cried out and clutched his chest. "My heart." He staggered backward and doubled over, not quite falling but crumbling around himself.

Skinny's attention shifted just long enough for Stanley to pull his hand out of his pocket. Brass knuckles engraved with power-enhancing runes glimmered on Stanley's hand. He took a swing that would have made Muhammed Ali proud. The force of the uppercut lifted the vampire to his toes.

Burke ran all out toward the hairy guy with Gordon on her tail. The kid recovered, heading straight toward Stanley, who stood in a wide-legged fighting stance.

Richard yanked a pistol from a holster under his jacket and fired six quick rounds at the vampire. Two of them hit the mark, doing virtually no damage but succeeding in stopping him.

"Stake," Stanley yelled.

From the corner of her eye, Burke saw a wooden stake flying end-over-end through the air, and then she was launching herself at the second vampire, who was only an arm's length away from her grandfather.

The force of the impact was enough to knock the wind out of her. The vampire put his arms under her legs and flipped her up over his shoulder like she weighed no more than a rag doll. Upside down, driven by pure adrenaline, Burke slammed the stake into the center of his back in the instant before she landed badly on the pavement. Her left shoulder took the brunt of the fall. Something snapped inside, wrenching an ugly guttural noise from her. She rolled onto her side as Gordon drove a second stake home from the front side.

His must have hit the mark more effectively than hers. Hairy fell to his knees in a spreading pool of blood next to skinny, who'd already flattened into a nauseating puddle of flesh and fluid.

Burke struggled to her knees, and Gordon's arms were around her, lifting gently, helping her up to her feet. "How bad?" he asked.

Stanley passed them at a quick trot. Along the road, the rumble of an eighteen-wheeler was growing closer.

"Bad enough," she said through clenched teeth. "Broken collar bone, maybe?"

"The drivers are both drained," Stanley said, returning from the side of the building where Burke had noticed the diesel pumps.

"Somebody's coming," Richard said.

Stanley took Burke's face in his hands. "We've got to get out of here."

"It's not fatal. Let's roll." Not fatal, but damn it hurt. She leaned hard against Gordon and let him tuck her into the back seat of the Cadillac.

Sans headlights, Stanley tore out of the gas station parking lot and raced northward. In the side view mirror, twin LEDs materialized behind them, grew brighter, then turned into the station.

"Hunters are led to the hunt, eh?" Gordon asked.

"More often than not," Stanley said, switching the lights on at last and slowing to a demure three miles over the speed limit.

"It would have been helpful for those truckers if we'd been led an hour earlier."

"It will have to be enough that we saved the one who's there now."

Richard crossed his arms over his sunken chest. "Dang it, I really needed to use the sandbox. How far to the next stop?"

"Ten miles. Maybe fifteen," Stanley told him.

Burke closed her eyes and focused on breathing. Stanley was being cocky. Her grandfather was complaining. Gordon's gentle hand brushed over her hair.

Everything's fine. It wasn't even a fair fight. They never stood a chance. Everything's fine. Everyone's safe. Repeating the mantra in her mind wasn't enough to stop the tremors that came. *I could have lost them all just like that.* Nothing scared her more.

CHAPTER FOUR

Richard

BY THE TIME THE CITYSCAPE OF GREATER PORTLAND sprouted up around them, the sun poured its fire out into the Pacific on the Cadillac's left.

As they drove north, one eye on the rearview mirror for cops, Stanley told them he planned to stop. It wasn't wise to head into the untamed portion of the state unrested, especially at night. It wouldn't hurt Burke to rest in a real bed, either.

At the memory of her tortured scream when Stanley reset her bone while pulled off on the shoulder of the highway, Richard's guts churned like he'd spent the day snacking on hot peppers and whiskey. She was asleep now, stoned on pills Stanley shook out of a white plastic bottle.

The Holiday Inn Express squatted next to yet another truck stop. It wasn't anything fancy, but it was clean. The hotel took cash payment, and the cafe next door had a sign out front advertising pie. Good enough for him. He wondered if they had prune juice. If not, he might need to swing by a grocer in the morning. The burger and fries hadn't done him any favors, and it wouldn't do to head into a big hunt with his bowels tied in a knot.

The three of them dragged their bags and a half-conscious Burke into the hotel through a side door to avoid the curious eyes of the front desk staff. Her room had a single bed large enough to sleep all four of them shoulder-to-shoulder. Richard pulled the covers back. Gordon lowered her onto the mattress as gentle as a mother with a newborn babe, and Stanley tugged the pink and white sneakers off her feet.

A door across from Burke's bathroom let them access a second room without returning to the hall and fiddling with the electronic locks.

Richard eyed the two double beds warily. "You going to make the new guy sleep on the floor?"

Stanley and Gordon exchanged a look in which Richard saw volumes spoken. Not understanding it made him feel stupid and grouchy.

"What?" he demanded.

"This room is for you and me, Dick," Stanley said.

Richard looked back at the open door to Burke's room and then at Gordon. Understanding clicked on like a cartoon light-bulb over his head. How was he supposed to know? Things weren't done that way in his time.

"Used to be different," he muttered.

"Very true." Stanley unzipped his duffle and withdrew a leather shaving bag. "If you'll excuse me." He disappeared into the bathroom, leaving Richard alone with Gordon.

Had they ever been alone together before? Richard couldn't remember. He was loath to lay on the bed in his dirty clothes, so he pulled the desk chair out and plopped down with an involuntary groan. It took the television a long time to turn on, and when it did, an advertisement for the hotel played. Seemed kind of stupid to waste resources advertising a thing to people who already bought it. Gordon settled in the small, low sofa that Richard had avoided for fear of not being able to get himself out again.

He ought to tell him hurting his granddaughter was a one-way ticket to broken kneecaps or at least ask what his intentions were, but when it came to Burke, such subjects felt like shifting sand beneath his feet. Burke would take the guy's knees out before Richard could, and she'd deduced his intentions before she agreed to a first date. Stuck in indecision, he opted to say nothing and switched the television to the local news.

A pretty bottle-blonde with blue eyes cold as ice and twinkling with poorly disguised excitement stared out at them in larger-than-life high definition. "…incident marks the third incident of the mysterious illness to strike in the rural coastline areas of the Olympic Peninsula. Officials interviewed had no comment and said that the boy is in critical condition."

The camera switched angles. The blonde turned her head and swapped expressions like a person changing shirts. "With the coming election, voters are wondering where the candidates stand on the issue of—"

Richard hit the mute button and spun the chair in Gordon's direction. "What do you make of Stanley saying old Busar's a lost cause?" Gordon regarded him seriously. So far as Richard could tell, the guy did everything seriously.

"You all talk about the lore. I barely know what that means. My opinion is pretty worthless when it comes to hunting."

"Opinions are like armpits," Richard told him. "Everybody's got two, and most of them stink. I'd still like to hear yours." The whole subject refused to stop eating at him. Why was Stanley being stubborn as a bunion when it came to their ideas? It wasn't like him. He'd never even really answered Richard's question. What made Busar's situation so different from Stanley's? If they saved Stan, couldn't they also patch up the old guy?

Some men carried the military with them for life. They might leave active duty, but their bearing, their posture, the way they talked, ate, made their beds, and folded their socks all screamed soldier. No one with eyes would miss the obvious fact that Gordon had served. He took his time to answer and chose his words with care.

"During my first tour, there was this call that came in—some village on the edge of nowhere needed help. There wasn't even a real road going out there. We went in Humvees, digging trails through the dust. Six vehicles. By the time we figured out it was a trap, only two remained. We all told ourselves those guys were dead. Somebody knocked on doors and told the wives and mothers."

"It happens, right? That's the hell of it," Richard said.

"Yeah, it happens. That's what made it an easy story to sell." A person could have mistaken the man for a lifelike statue if not for the single index finger tapping against the arm of the sofa. "Thing is, we never went back and looked for those boys. We were in no man's land. It was hell on earth. A little kid with big brown eyes would walk up to you and ask for water. When you tried to hand it to him, he'd chuck a grenade into camp. Nobody trusted anybody. Guys screamed in the night because of what they'd seen. It wasn't the kind of stuff they put on the six o'clock news back in the land of prosperity. It was the kind of stuff that leaves veterans sitting on the street corner, drinking rotgut, and talking to voices no one else can hear."

Richard wondered what this had to do with Stanley, but he knew better than to interrupt. He waited while Gordon stared at a scene playing out for him and him alone.

"Three, four months later, this kid came staggering out of the desert, burned to hell, more dead than alive from dehydration and whatever came before that. Doubt he was even old enough to buy his own beer yet. I don't know how he had the strength to make it. I don't think I could have. He told us they'd been taken alive, for the most part." At last, Gordon's gaze met Richard's. "With that kid standing right there in front of him, the CO shook his head and said, 'I'm sorry to tell you, soldier, but those men are dead, and they're not coming back.'"

A gust of wind howled past the window, and Richard shivered like the winter air had blown through the middle of him.

"Sometimes, it's a whole lot easier to believe a person's dead than to consider what a rescue might cost," Gordon whispered.

Stanley came out of the bathroom in a swirl of hot steam. "Has anyone ordered dinner yet? I'm famished."

Richard hauled his old body out of the chair with a groan that came out of someplace deep inside his bone marrow. "I'll let you do it. I'm going to shower, too."

No matter how hot the water ran, he couldn't quite thaw the chill Gordon's story had left inside him.

CHAPTER FIVE

Ben

BEN'S EYES SNAPPED OPEN. THE GROGGINESS AND STIFFNESS of falling asleep on the couch left him as quickly as water down a drain. Stanley was getting close. He knew it. The certainty hummed in his veins.

Maybe he'd knock on Loretta's door and beg for help. Not right away, though. How many times had he heard about Stanley being fancy, Stanley being proper, Stanley being dapper? Enough to make a man sick. He'd stop somewhere to freshen up if he was traveling before showing up at Loretta's doorstep.

There were half a dozen small motels in town, but none of them were anywhere near as decent as The Quillayute River Resort. Ben pulled their number up on his phone and asked the woman who answered if they had a reservation for Stanley Kapcheck.

"No, sir, I don't see anyone by that name," she replied.

Ben balled his left hand into a fist, squeezing the corner of a pillow to vent some of his ire and prevent it from coming out in his voice. "I'm sorry to be a pest, but the reservation might not be under Stanley's name. He's a dear friend of my mother's. I'd really love to surprise him. It might be under the name of his traveling companion, but I'm not sure what that is. They'll be coming in from–"

"I wish I could help you," she cut in. "But this time of year, hardly anyone is coming in. We've got four reservations on the books, and they're all folks who've stayed here before. No Stanley Kapcheck."

Not bothering with the nonsense of meaningless niceties, Ben hung up and thought about it. Would he stay at that B&B? No way. Too personal. A hunter would want his space.

Space.

Yes!

His fingers flew across the screen, and in seconds a man had answered with a gruff hello.

"Is this the store that has those little cabins out back for rent?" Ben demanded.

"What can I do for you?" a gruff male voice answered.

He opened his mouth to dish out the story about his mother's friend, but the second before the words spilled out, he realized that asking those questions might lead the proprietor to spill the beans to Stanley. That wouldn't do at all. What a blessing that the first hotel had been a bust. He'd nearly made a monumental mistake.

"I have a friend coming into town sometime in the next few days, and he's going to need a place to stay. I was thinking of your cabins, but my neighbor told me you're full all the time."

The guy cackled like a cartoon character. "Full? That's a good one. I got nobody. One guy's supposed to be coming in tomorrow, but if it weren't for him, I'd close it up and sleep the week away on the cot in the back room."

Bingo.

Ben hung up without further fuss, gripped with the

certainty that it was Stanley. If he was coming tomorrow, that left just enough time to get ready.

Finding the necessary items and performing the spell took almost two hours. By the time he finished, his mother was calling him for dinner. She'd made spaghetti again. When he finally managed to get rid of her, he would never eat spaghetti another day, but working left him too hungry to spurn her pathetic effort. He had to eat quickly before sunset. No one in their right mind would wander the forest after dark, and he had work to do.

MASTERING THE ART OF SCRYING HAD TAKEN MONTHS, BUT thanks to his exceptional talent, Ben figured it out. He knew precisely where the monster's lair was. He didn't expect the pain that struck him when he got close, as if the sun was burning his skin to the point of blistering.

He staggered back a few steps, and the discomfort diminished immediately.

He wasn't the only one working magic in this part of the forest.

"Dammit, I don't have time for this."

Already, the world had drawn a blanket of deep shadows over itself, and he still had to get back to the road before full dark.

Was this close enough?

It was going to have to be. Sometimes the key to success was being able to adapt.

"*Veni ad me.*" He spoke with authority, hands out like St. Francis of Assisi, welcoming the forest creatures.

Creatures of lesser intelligence were powerless against his authority. They came, insects buzzing through the air, worms burrowing out of the earth at his command. Birds fluttered down from their hidden perches to land at his feet. Chipmunks skittered through the undergrowth to obey him. Three deer trotted out of the shadows. A bear approached the outer part of the ring of beasts.

Ben squatted and held his hand out to a fat brown squirrel. "*Veni ad me*," he whispered. Trembling, the creature stepped into his master's hand. Its tiny heart raced within its breast with such ferocity that it vibrated against Ben's palm. "Consider it a mercy. You don't want to be around for what's to come."

He carried his prey to a hole he'd dug. The other animals scattered. Now that his attention was no longer focused on them, nothing held them to the spot. When he wrenched the small head from the body, warm blood poured over his hands and dripped onto the crystal and the herbs he'd set out.

"*Et in hoc loco. Tu imperio meo non potest resistere*," Ben chanted.

He picked up a razor blade he'd left on the ground with his equipment, cut the squirrel's chest open, and extracted the still heart. No bigger than the tip of his finger, the organ was slick and difficult to hold on to. He placed it with care in the hole, covered the heart, then pressed both hands to the spot.

With utmost caution, he opened the veil and let the magic do its work. The power poured out of him, taking his energy with it, but more than that, taking pieces of himself. He let them go, happy to give them in service of the greater good.

Closing the curtain was harder than usual, so difficult that, for a split second, he worried he'd lost control, but then it was done. He sat on the cold earth, panting, the sweat on his skin chilling him in the cool night air.

Get up, Ben. Get out of here.

He pushed himself to his feet and staggered back to his car on watery legs, grinning. He'd done well. Everything was coming together.

CHAPTER SIX

Richard

One of the best parts about hanging out with Stanley and Burke was that there seemed to be an endless supply of money. None of them threw the cash around needlessly, but nobody stopped to ask where the next meal would come from. Richard had earned a respectable salary during his days at Wellington Plastics, but there had always been a need to keep an accounting of each dollar, lest he fall short and not be able to provide for his daughter. But now he lived a life where cash was plucked from the branches of a tree always in bloom. He didn't ask where it came from. It was enough that it was there.

They skipped the powdered eggs and plastic-wrapped muffins in the hotel's common room and piled in the Caddy to drive to the cafe. On a warm summer day, it would have been a pleasant stroll. With the winter wind whipping their clothes around their half-frozen bodies, it seemed wiser to drive.

Inside, the cafe smelled of fresh-baked pie and bacon. Richard's mouth watered the second the heavenly aroma reached him.

"You got prune juice?" he asked the waitress, a rhino of a woman with her hair piled on top of her head and held in place by some force his mind couldn't conceive of. The immense tower of curls added at the better part of a foot to her already substantial height.

She chomped on a piece of gum like a cow chewing cud, but she shoved the wad into her cheek to answer him. "Yup. Prune, grape, orange, grapefruit, and some banana mango concoction with more sugar than liquid."

"Just a glass of prune juice and a cup of coffee." He turned his attention to the menu.

Stanley ordered coffee, and the two health nuts asked for ice water. Who could start a day with ice water? A body needed a bit of sugar and caffeine to kick it into gear. Anybody playing with a full deck knew that much.

Stanley had grabbed a newspaper from a machine outside the restaurant. While the rest of them focused on deciding what to order, he scanned the pages of the thin publication.

Narrowing his choices down to the cinnamon pecan French toast or corned beef hash with eggs, Richard wondered if he should flip a coin to decide. *I could order both and just eat half of each. No, too wasteful.*

"Look at this." Stanley folded the paper into a neat rectangle and dropped it on the polished tabletop next to a wire rack of jellies and sauces.

The waitress plodded up to the table and thunked their drinks down. Her gasp drew the attention of the entire group. "Isn't that just terrible?" With one hand pressed to her titanic bosom, she pointed at the newspaper with the other. "Those poor babies. You ask me, the government's messing around up there."

Richard stole a glance at the headline.

Mystery Illness Claims Third Victim

"Why do you think it's the government?" Burke asked.

A shake of the head did nothing to unsettle the column of curls. Her red-painted lips twisted into a sneer. "I tell you, there's a whole lot of land up there that nobody puts on maps, and more weird comes out of that forest than the rest of this continent combined. If it's not the government, I'll eat my girdle."

Richard grimaced at the thought of the gargantuan woman's girdle.

"I heard two more kids got it," she went on. "No connection to each other, either. They're up in Forks, out on the Quileute Res, one of them was living illegally out in the forest in a camper. Parents brought her into Seattle General, and there wasn't a thing they could do."

"You're following this story pretty closely," Gordon observed.

"I got seven babies of my own at home. You think I don't know when something's out there that might hurt my angels? Of course, Donella's old enough that the apron strings have been cut for some time, but little Georgina doesn't even have the sense not to eat her own boogers yet."

Richard's hearty appetite was draining away quick as a striped lizard on hot pavement.

"You seem to be a step ahead of the local news," Stanley said.

The rhino woman grunted. "A man with no legs would be a step ahead of that rag, but I've got a cousin who's a state trooper. I hear things the general public isn't yet savvy to."

A man in a cheap navy-blue suit banged his cup on his table. "Could we get some more coffee over here?"

She threw a look over her shoulder that resulted in instant silence. If the gruff customer had been a dog, his tail would've been tucked up to his underside.

The waitress returned her attention to the hunters. "Youz decide what you want yet?"

"Certainly, I'll have the bagel and a bowl of cottage cheese," Stanley said.

Burke ordered a cup of fruit, and Gordon asked for wheat toast and turkey bacon with his eggs.

So much for ordering double just for enjoyment's sake. It would be impossible to enjoy a feast like that when everyone else ate like a bunch of frail old ladies. But which to choose?

"I'll have the corned beef with two eggs over medium." He could already taste the hot saltiness in his imagination, and he congratulated himself for his choice.

A man as diminutive as their waitress was enormous scurried past the table carrying a tray upon which three plates heaped up with French toast, soaked in syrup, topped with whipped cream and pecans.

Richard's stomach growled. "Hold on, I think I'd rather—"

But she'd already bulldozed her way back through the kitchen door.

"What's up, grandpa?" Burke asked.

"Nothing." He drank his prune juice to avoid being accused of looking pouty. Sometimes a man just had to accept his lot in life.

It must have worked because Burke dropped the subject and pulled the paper between her and Gordon and they spent the next minute or two reading the details. "What do you make of this?" she asked.

"It's too many deaths, too close together for a"—Stanley glanced around to make sure no one was listening—"for what I told you about."

"And you're still discounting the possibility of an illness?" Burke asked.

"This is hunter's work. I'd stake my life on it," Stanley said.

That was a stupid choice of words. Weren't they all staking their lives on those bets every time they walked into a mess like this?

"How is a boogeyman created?" Gordon asked.

Stanley shook his head. "They just *are*. As far as I know, whatever is here now is what's been here forever."

"Not like a werewolf or some other creatures that can change a human?" Gordon said.

Stanley shook his head. "I've never heard of such a thing among the truly ancient."

Richard polished off his juice. "You say that a lot, Stan Kapcheck, but we've found out you ain't heard of half of what is."

"Have I ever claimed otherwise?" Stanley asked.

CHAPTER SEVEN

Burke

IF SHE HAD TO GUESS, BURKE WOULD SAY THAT SHE'D traveled more than the average American. She'd seen the twinkling lights of Paris and smelled the canals of Venice. When she and Greg got married, they visited Niagara Falls and Disney World, went to Marti Gras in New Orleans, and spent one memorable Christmas in New York City. Since joining up with her grandfather and Stanley, she'd crisscrossed the country in the Cadillac until her butt felt permanently seat-shaped. For all that, she'd never seen the Pacific Northwest.

As they drove northwest toward the Olympic Peninsula, the trappings of civilization fell away until they were on a narrow blacktop road beneath a canopy of moss-covered trees so immense it formed an alien sky of green dappled with gold. Ferns as tall as a man and three times as wide filled the gaps between tree trunks large enough to drive through. Mist swirled across the land. No matter that the clock read mid-day and the sun blazed in a cloudless sky—in this place, the earth existed in a state of perpetual twilight.

"I feel like a dinosaur's going to walk out of this forest," Gordon mumbled.

It would be easy to believe modern society was a dream here. Mankind was just another species of beast existing on an untamed planet. Beneath the behemoth trees, humans were no more than another tiny insect scrambling about in the undergrowth.

Adding to the sensation of being dwarfed by her surroundings, the road occasionally took them to the edge of the continent. There, the earth plummeted in sheer rock to the rolling gray sea that raged against the land again and again, sending plumes of salt water into the sky.

Burke shifted in her seat. Her left shoulder ached despite the pills she'd taken and the sling Stanley had picked up for her at a drug store back in the city. She pulled the right sleeve of her hoodie down over her hand to warm it.

"I don't think I've ever used this word before, but this is awesome," Gordon said.

Awesome. Inspiring awe. Yes, that was a good description, but she couldn't decide if she loved it or hated it. She feared it. The waitress's voice echoed in her memory.

"I tell you, there's a whole lot of land up there that nobody puts on maps, and more weird comes out of that forest than the rest of this continent combined."

"Stanley, what's the plan when we get to the hotel?" Talking was better than crawling further inside her own over-active imagination. She had to take action, but not much a person could do while traveling four to a vehicle.

"It's not a hotel, per se. More like a cluster of cabins," he replied. "The spot is lovely. The front porches overlook the sea, and the forest grows adjacent to little gardens in the back yards. Of course, this time of year, there won't be much in the gardens, but I imagine it will be cozy, no matter."

Based on his description, cozy wasn't the word that came to mind,

Burke pressed him to answer the question.

"I've given it a great deal of thought since our unforeseen adventure at the truck stop the other evening. I'm known, but in no place am I known like I am up here."

"Because this is monster territory," Richard said.

Apparently, he'd been thinking about it, too.

"Indeed."

A dark shape moved in the shadows, deep in the forest alongside the road. A moose? A bear? Something more sinister? Was it moving alongside the car or according to its own agenda?

Get a grip, girl.

"So, what does that mean?" she asked.

"I think it would be best if the three of you took point on investigating in town. Perhaps I could spend the first day making some calls and running the operation from the cabin," Stanley said.

"We taking the FBI route?" Richard asked.

Despite her inner heebie-jeebies, his question drew a smidgen of a smile from her. Her grandfather always complained about being forced to wear a suit and tie, but he obviously loved flashing an FBI badge and commanding the respect of the people he interviewed.

"I was thinking CDC," Stanley said.

"Do we have identification for that?" Burke asked.

"Give me a few minutes once we get to the cabin. I can work something up that'll pass."

"Do you all ever think about how much trouble you'd be in if you ever got caught with all these fake IDs?" Gordon asked.

Burke couldn't help but laugh along with Richard, who broke into great guffaws.

"Yeah! That's our biggest worry," he gasped, tears rolling down his cheeks.

Gordon had the good grace to shrug and chuckle along with them.

People said there was no such thing as a stupid question, but people were wrong about a great many things.

AROUND NOON, STANLEY PARKED IN A GRAVEL LOT THAT WAS little more than a wide spot on the shoulder of the serpentine road. Since he was trying to keep a low profile, Burke and Gordon went inside to check in. The building was narrow as a house trailer, with the widest part facing the road. Windows across the back looked out over a pioneer village of log cabins— six, that she could see—and beyond them, the sea rolled on and on and on.

In the center of the single large foyer, a horseshoe-shaped counter served as a reception desk. To the left, a small selection of groceries, toiletries, and personal items filled three glass-front refrigerators and half a dozen low shelves. To the right, racks of t-shirts, shot glasses, and backpacks bore the state's name in a variety of styles.

A man no more than five feet tall with a beard so thick and long it gave the impression of being solely responsible for his hunched posture greeted them with a picket-fence grin. "Not a lot of visitors this time of year. Cold and rainy is a relief to the outsiders in the summertime, but it's what they're trying to escape from in the winter. Not many're content with what they got when they get it."

"I think it's stunning up here," Gordon said.

"You think right. Only some people can't see it because they got their head up their backside and they can't hear it 'cause their cheeks are covering their ears."

Burke fumbled one-handed in her wallet, wiggled her real

driver's license out of the pocket, and slid it across the counter. "We've heard there are kids getting sick up here."

A split-second hesitation in copying Burke's information onto a postcard-sized rental agreement ruined the man's lie. "Not sure what you're talking about."

"That's why we came here, actually. Some people have all the luck, and I guess this time it's us because we get to come to this extraordinary place, but it's not leisure that brings us. We're with the CDC."

The man returned Burke's ID and dropped a key on a purple rectangular keychain onto the counter. "Don't know what that means. Everybody talks in initials nowadays."

"The Center for Disease Control," Burke said. "We investigate potentially dangerous outbreaks."

A twitch of the man's diminutive form might have passed for a shrug. "I ain't had so much as a cold in forty years, and I ain't so much of a busy body as to be asking after anybody else's health, so I guess I don't know nothing about any diseases."

"So, you haven't heard about the sick children?" Burke pressed. "We saw an article in the paper back in Portland."

"Young people now days are soft. Scared of their own shadows. Got a pill for everything. Kids get sick. My own three had green boogers on their faces more days than not, no matter how hard the old lady tried to keep 'em clean. Don't see how the government's going to put an end to that."

"To be honest," Burke said, "we don't know either, but we're going to try."

"I wish you luck then, lady. You got your pick, but I put you in cabin three. It's got the best water pressure."

They thanked him, took the key, and joined Richard and Stanley in investigating their temporary lodgings.

On a cliff, fifty feet above the susurrating sea, cabin number three boasted a weathered front porch with two unattractive but sturdy-looking rocking chairs. Inside, a tiny bedroom flanked each side of the small, combined living area and kitchen. A single bath the size of the average closet had been tacked on as an afterthought. Soft braided rugs covered the floor in oval patches. Glass-front cabinets held sturdy white dishes.

Under other circumstances, Burke could imagine settling into the cozy cabin for a relaxing vacation. As it was, she eyed the meager two bars on her cell phone and hoped they'd maintain a good enough connection to stay in contact with one another and operate a hotspot for research purposes.

Gordon carried her duffle and dropped it on the bed in the room to the left of the single kitchen counter. She unzipped it and fished out the pain pills Stanley had given her.

"Bad?" Gordon asked.

"Less than good," Burke said. "Don't worry about it. I'll be fine."

He ran a gentle hand along the slope of her back. "I do worry about it. I want you to be well."

By the time they returned to the main room, Stanley had already unpacked a box of books and a laptop computer on the sturdy round dining table. "I'm going to try to see if I can pull any information out of Forks Police Department."

"Why would the cops keep a record on a sick kid?" Richard asked.

"It's worth a shot. Why don't the rest of you change clothes and head into town?"

Burke did her best to get the wrinkles out of her clothes with the tiny steamer she carried. No way she would be able to wrestle herself into a pair of tights, but it was too cold for a dress anyway, so she settled for black slacks and a simple blouse, both of which she managed with a minimum of pain. To give credit where credit was due, that probably had more to do with the large white pills than with any exceptional fortitude she possessed. The downside of the drugs was that the world kept swimming in front of her eyes while she tried to smudge on eyeliner and lipstick.

"You look woozy," Gordon said when she emerged from the bathroom.

"I'm fine," she lied. She was woozy. Her stomach rolled.

"Rest," Gordon said. "I'll go with your grandpa. We're just asking questions. Broad daylight. Not even a full moon. We'll be fine."

A powerful urge to protest couldn't quite pass the gray haze induced by the drugs. "At least it doesn't hurt right now."

He smiled, slow and sexy, and she fell deeper in love with him. "I'm glad for that."

Leaving the explanations to Gordon, she wandered back into the bedroom and crawled under the faded quilt without bothering to change into more comfortable clothes. In the moment before sleep claimed her, the front door shut, and she hoped broad daylight and the lack of a full moon would be enough to keep the two men safe.

CHAPTER EIGHT

Ben

By parking in the restaurant lot and walking a quarter mile, Ben managed to hide quite well. Concealed behind a pile of old crates and rusty propane tanks, he had a clear view of the enormous Cadillac and a half-blocked view of the cabin door. No one would be able to see him from either the cabin or the office windows. When the cabin door swung open with a squeak that reached his ears, even at that distance, he leaned as far over as he dared to catch a glimpse of Stanley Kapcheck. Unfortunately, he only caught a glimpse of two figures shrouded in warm winter hats and coats ducking into the car. Once the doors closed, all he could see was the reflection of the drifting clouds in the windows.

Who else could be in the room but Stanley Kapcheck? Had Stanley found some poor sap to be his protégé, just as Busar had found Stanley? Most likely. Too bad the sucker was going to get caught in the fallout. Then again, wouldn't the entire planet get caught in the fallout, eventually? May as well join the group early. Party like it's 1999 and all that rot.

He forced himself to wait until the rumble of the big V8 engine had died away in the distance, then darted to the porch of the cabin. The hex bag didn't need to be well hidden; it just needed to be tucked well enough out of sight that when the hunters returned, they wouldn't notice it before they climbed the steps. Then, the moment they moved past it, the spell would be triggered, and the games would begin. Everything led up to this point. Shit was about to get real. So thrilling was the notion that his body responded in a most surprising way.

Hmm. Maybe there'd be time to stop at one of the local bars to find a girl up for some quick, no-frills romance. He strolled back to his car, wondering if Stanley spotted him watching the highway from the forest. There was no real reason to make a point of watching the car rolling into town, but he wanted to verify that the hunter of legend was a man and not just a myth.

Between that excursion and this one, he was ready to put his feet up, but there was one more chore to attend to. It wouldn't do for the mystery that drew Stanley to town to disappear before everything had played out to the conclusion Ben planned. Sadly, for the kiddos, more energy would have to be sapped away. Sadder still, it would likely be the last time for one or two of them.

Then again, everybody had to go some time. Really, he was granting them a gift, freeing them from this earthly prison while they still believed that life was good and full of possibility. All that with the added benefit of making his mother's dearest wish come true.

You're a saint. No, you're more than that. You're a god.

He pulled his keys from his pocket and pressed the unlock button on the fob. In the distance, his car chirped in response. The prospect of victory battled with his exhaustion. Shaking his head, he laughed to himself. So many people to kill, so little time.

CHAPTER NINE

Richard

GORDON DROVE THE CADILLAC LIKE HE WAS TRYING TO prove something on the track in Indianapolis. Stanley drove fast. Gordon raced, and the virile purr of the well-tuned engine brought a smile to Richard's face. No denying the Caddy was one of the most beautiful pieces of machinery ever to grace the American highway.

"Stanley said he was going to call out to the clinic up in Forks. One of the doctors out there was quoted by the press as having said one of the kids was a patient of hers. Forks Hospital is just around the corner from there. We might ask around there, too."

"I thought these kids were spread out all over the place."

"Not a lot of choices for medical care in the rainforest, not even when the rainforest is part of modern America."

The clinic looked more like a rustic hotel than a medical center, in Richard's opinion, but the inside was clean and welcoming, and the lady at the front desk greeted them with a smile.

"You must be the investigators from the CDC?"

Both flashed the plastic badges Stanley had made up while they'd been getting dressed. "I'm Agent Westchester; this is my associate, Agent Bell."

She nodded, and a mass of glossy red curls bounced around her shoulders. "Your associate called a few minutes ago to let us know you were coming. If you don't mind taking a seat, Dr. Escobar will be out after she's finished with her patient."

They took a seat in the row of white plastic armchairs. Richard approved of white plastic in a doctor's office. It was impossible to hide nasty stains on white, and plastic was easy to bleach. Gordon stared straight ahead as if he were watching a movie no one else could see.

Richard scanned the flyers arranged in neat stacks on the coffee table in front of him. One for alcoholics, one for pregnant women, and one for people with depression. Whatever happened to keeping a stock of good old Reader's Digest magazines so a man could feed his brain while he waited? Nowadays, everyone stares at their phone screens while they sit. He'd wasted half a lifetime staring at a screen, entertaining his hours away. Richard's stomach grumbled. He wished he'd stuck a granola bar or something in his pocket. Although, the cute redhead would probably tell him off for eating in a doctor's office.

At last, the door opened, and an elderly woman with dark skin, dark eyes, and even darker circles underneath them emerged. Her white lab coat hung from drooping shoulders. Beneath it, she wore a shapeless gray dress. The only spot of color on her whole body was the bright red stethoscope draped around her neck. She held out a hand nearly as small as a child's, and both men shook it.

"Thank you for making the time to see us today," Gordon said.

"I don't imagine I'll be much help, but I'm glad to know

someone, somewhere, is paying attention to these kinds of things. Come on back to my office."

Richard and Gordon sat in padded chairs and the doctor situated herself behind the desk, which was neither grand nor shabby. This place wasn't half bad. If Richard lived here, he'd be perfectly happy visiting this office for his medical needs.

"Are you medical doctors?" the woman asked.

"No, ma'am. We're investigators. If we find sufficient cause for worry, we will call in folks with medical expertise," Gordon said. He was pretty good at this for a new guy.

"How does one investigate medical issues if one is not a medical expert?"

Richard willed himself not to fidget while Gordon ran the show.

"Our training is broad, doctor. We know how to spot people and situations that do not fit the normal patterns."

"Do you have a warrant of some kind?"

"No, ma'am. We're just asking a few questions."

The thin slash of the doctor's mouth twitched, but she didn't press the issue. "And exactly how can I help you?"

"We understand that you treated one of the children who fell ill."

"I treated two of them," the doctor replied. "The parents made that a matter of public knowledge, so I don't mind mentioning it."

Gordon shifted and stretched his back.

It gave Richard a tidbit of satisfaction to see that the younger, fitter man also struggled to get the kinks out after multiple days stuffed inside a vehicle.

When Gordon continued, he asked, "Can you tell us what their disease looked like? Symptoms? How quickly it progressed?"

She met Gordon's gaze. "If you're investigators for the American medical community, then you should know that I cannot tell you that. The patient's privacy is protected unless a court orders me to disclose personal information."

"Of course," Gordon said. "We're not asking you to violate ethics. We're asking for what you can tell us—any information at all that will help us understand what's happening here."

She chewed on that for a while, probably looking for traps that might get her in trouble. In Richard's opinion, life would be easier for everybody if there weren't so many doggone laws about every nitpicking thing. Who cared if a dead person's symptoms got leaked to the public? Not the dead person, that was for certain.

At last, she folded her hands on the desk blotter. She held Richard's gaze for a long moment and then Gordon's. "This is what I will say about the deaths of the children in this area. Your visit here strikes me as odd. I believe you probably are *some kind* of government agents, but something tells me you're not telling us the whole story. That's fine. Governments have kept secrets as long as the concept of government has existed. It's the way of the world, and I'm not the woman to fight the system. But I get a strange feeling from you two. I don't feel entirely safe, and I'm not sure if it's because of you or because of something else entirely. I believe that there is a danger that is lurking that I can't quite make out. I may not be an investigator, but I am a physician. It's my job to pay attention to the details to diagnose the larger problems. I may not have the answer yet, but I know when I'm on the right track."

Richard understood what she meant. He'd also felt that sensation of having the oldest part of his brain—the part that learned to run far and fast at unexpected noises—wake up and pay attention even when he didn't know why.

Didn't mean he had to like hearing it from her.

Richard scooted forward in his chair and opened his mouth to argue, but the untrusting doctor silenced him with a glare from her obsidian eyes.

"Something is weird about this visit, and it's not the first time in recent months I've had that sensation," she said.

Richard looked over at Gordon, who appeared entranced once again by whatever was right in front of him. After a moment, he focused directly on the little woman commanding their meeting. "Let's talk about you, doctor. No ethical violation there. Have you lived in this area your whole life?"

"Except for a few years in my youth when I traveled and attended university, yes."

"So, it's safe to say you've established strong ties to the community, the people who live up here with you."

She sat up straighter and narrowed her eyes, as if Gordon's questioning sparked hope and wariness. "I have."

"You've treated people of all ages, correct?"

"I have."

What the Sam Hill was Gordon getting at? Did they need to know the doctor's life story? Weren't they supposed to be finding out about the children? But Gordon seemed thrilled by the answers he'd gotten.

Gordon's leg bounced up and down. He said, "I haven't spent much time here yet, but I've heard a great deal about the area. There are many people groups represented on this peninsula, aren't there? Multiple races, each with their own unique customs and probably different medical needs as well, according to those customs and their ancestral DNA."

She leaned in toward him, the hint of a smile on her saggy face. "That is an astute observation."

"How long have you practiced medicine here?"

"I began at Forks Hospital in the 1970s. I've been at this clinic for almost thirty years now."

"You must have seen all manner of injuries and illnesses in that time."

"I'd say so, though any family practice doctor will tell you the majority of our time is given to strep throat and influenza, broken bones, and so forth." She scooted to the edge of her seat, waiting for whatever he asked next.

Richard scratched his head and tried to pat his unruly hair back down.

"And probably, because of the unusual nature of this part of the world, you've come to understand ailments other doctors have never even heard of," Gordon said.

"Perhaps."

"Now, I'm not talking specifically about the children you treated here, but given the public information that's been shared on the news—the fatigue, wasting away, the age of the victims, and so on, have you ever seen anything like this?"

The doctor seemed to weigh her words before she answered. "A long time ago, I came across similar symptoms. Those children passed on, with one exception. Never before or since have I seen or heard of any other cases."

"A young girl by the name of Christine suffered from this affliction maybe twenty, twenty-five years ago," Gordon said.

The doctor's hooded eyes widened, but she said nothing.

Gordon rose from his chair and reached across the desk. "You've been very helpful. Thank you."

She shook hands with Gordon, then released him and automatically extended her hand to Richard. "You know what this is, don't you?"

Gordon said, "We're getting closer to understanding."

"Are you really investigators with the CDC?"

He grimaced in his surly way, which was about as close to smiling as he ever seemed to come. "That's what it says on the badge."

The doctor walked them to the front door to let them out. Office hours had ended, and the receptionist had already locked up.

Her eyes fell on the Cadillac parked in front of the building. "It's a beautiful car," she said.

"Prettiest thing on the road," Richard agreed.

"I remember admiring one like it. That must have been, oh, twenty-five, thirty years ago."

Neither of the men replied to that, but once they'd passed into the chilly outdoors, she called out to them.

They turned to face her. She looked tiny and withered as a raisin, framed in the glass and steel doorway.

"Be careful out there, gentlemen. Folks around here enjoy their privacy. Tread lightly."

Gordon gave a curt nod, and they wasted no time getting out of the icy wind and into the car. The engine turned over so smoothly it was as if it had been impatiently waiting for them to return so they could devour a few more miles before sunset.

Though he'd resisted for a long time, Burke convinced Richard to carry a cell phone and keep it turned on. He peeked at the screen now and saw that Stanley had sent a message while they'd been talking to the doctor.

Dr. Dan Knife

Clallam County Medical Examiner

223 East Lakeside Ave., Port Angles

A second message read:

Chief of Police, Forks

Police Chief Jason Harper

5200 Evergreen St., Forks

Richard conveyed the information to Gordon.

"Let's see if we can catch the cop." Gordon shifted the car into reverse and backed out of the parking space. "Port Angeles must be more than an hour from here. Maybe we can go up there tomorrow."

"You want to tell me what all those questions were about back there?" Rickard asked.

"What do you mean?"

"I thought we were trying to get info about the kids."

"You could waterboard that woman, and she wouldn't break

her doctor/patient confidentiality." The way Gordon spoke made Richard feel like Gordon actually admired the woman's unreasonable stubbornness. That probably explained his attraction to Burke.

"I ain't blind," Richard muttered. "I got that, but what was with all the other stuff?"

They rolled to a stop light behind a twenty-year-old Ford Explorer and waited while three pick-up trucks and a Jeep rolled through on the cross street.

"Remember what Stanley told us about this part of the world being home to an unusual number of monsters?" Gordon asked.

"Well, I ain't senile if that's what you mean." If it had really been important, he would have remembered.

The light turned green Gordon proceeded through the intersection. "Well, I got to thinking about that back there. If there are more than the usual number of monster attacks up here, and that woman has been practicing medicine for an entire generation, she's seen some crazy stuff."

"And your point?"

"My point is that she would know the difference between human stuff and monster stuff. She wouldn't tell us anything about her patient, specifically, but she confirmed for us that, in her medical opinion, this isn't any kind of human sickness." He turned into the lot of a large white building with a metal roof. It looked more like part of a large-scale farming operation than a police station, but the sign out front told them they were in the right spot.

Richard harrumphed. He wasn't too sure about Gordon's logic. He'd have to think about it later. Right now, he had to go lie to the cops. It wasn't the life he thought he'd be living in his final years, but there was no denying it was exciting more often than not.

An old man with beetle-dark eyes set deep in a craggy face

sat on a bench watching them. His legs stretched out in front of him, hands folded over a belly that looked like he was about four months along. He brought to mind an elderly reptile basking in the sun. Except there was no sun, only a damp gray mist and a chilly salt-scented wind that, if he turned his head wrong, made Richard's hearing aid whistle annoyingly.

"I've seen that car before," the stranger said.

Pride swelled in Richard's heart. No one had ever noticed his old Toyota. "She's a beaut, ain't she?"

"You are not the owner," the man said.

It was like some folks didn't know how to have a proper conversation anymore.

"Do you know the owner?" Gordon asked.

"Does any man ever know another?"

"Come on," Richard said. "It's too cold to stand out here yapping." He hustled toward the front door of the building.

"Have you come for the children?" the man asked without turning to watch them go.

Gordon retreated toward the bench. "What are you talking about?"

"Have you come for the children?" he asked again.

"We've come to help them," Gordon said.

"You can't help."

"How do you know?"

"You can't even buy your own car. You have to drive someone else's."

This guy was just annoying.

"I'm going inside. We got real work to do here." Leaving Gordon to follow or not, Richard marched his old bones into the comfortable warmth of the municipal building.

CHAPTER TEN

Burke

BURKE OPENED HER EYES AND BLINKED UP AT THE WOOD-beam ceiling above her. A cheap fan spun in lazy circles above the bed, stirring the cool air, but she was snug and content beneath the heavy quilt. At least, she would have been content if not for the dull, throbbing ache in her left arm.

Suck it up, girl. Stanley got stabbed in the chest, and he didn't complain. You can deal with a bum shoulder for a few weeks.

That was true, but then again, Stanley benefited from the fantastic healing balm their friend made for them. They'd all enjoyed that stuff. Maybe it would have been wise to be a bit more judicious with its use when Nathanial told them he wouldn't be able to make any more for a long while. If she could rub some of that on her shoulder, she'd be right as rain and wouldn't even need the sling.

If a bull had batteries, his horns would blow, came to her in her grandfather's voice.

She shoved the covers off and climbed out of bed with a groan.

A lovely full-length mirror on a wooden stand reflected a less-than-lovely image. Burke's clothes looked rumpled and wilted as a flower stuffed in a child's pocket. The pillow left lines on the right side of her face. At least she didn't have to worry about bedhead anymore since she'd started cropping her hair almost to the scalp. Changing into yoga pants and a baggy sweatshirt sounded lovely, except that she knew it would aggravate her injury. *Stupid vampire.*

She found Stanley at the table, poring over a leather-bound book with crumbling yellow pages.

"How's the patient?" he asked.

"Grouchy. Do we have any coffee?"

"I believe Gordon unpacked the provisions in the kitchen."

She found a can of coffee grounds in one of the tidy glass-fronted cabinets; in another, a small pot that would brew one cup at a time. Working one-handed didn't do a thing to lift her mood.

Get your eyes off yourself, Burke. You're being a baby.

"Find anything useful?" she asked.

"Nothing I haven't seen many times before." Stanley sighed and closed the book, sending a tiny whirlwind of dust into the lamp-lit air like spirals of smoke curling lazily upward as they lifted the prayers of churchgoers toward the heavens.

"I confess, I'm at a complete loss. When Busar and I fought this monster on Christine's behalf, we had a powerful magical object. Nothing we have now comes close to the strength of that talisman. I have connections all over the world, but not one of them would be able to lay hands on something like that. If they did, they probably wouldn't want to, and even if they wanted to, I'd be a fool to try something again when it failed so spectacularly the first time."

The coffee pot whined like a cat stuck in a storm drain.

"I've read the lore about these bogeymen more times than I wish to recount," he said. "I read it before Busar, and I came here to hunt the creature. I read it in the years since. I read it just now while you were sleeping." His eyes twinkled. "Funny, no matter how many times I read it, nothing new ever appears."

"I can't believe they have no weakness," Burke said. "Even The Devil has weaknesses. There must be something. Besides, we don't even know for sure that's really what we're hunting."

Stanley ignored the second half of the statement and pounced on the first. "Humans have weaknesses, do they not?"

Burke rolled her eyes and gestured toward the sling pressing her arm against her chest.

"If an ant were to attack a human, would those weaknesses be in play?"

She took the way he asked it, his tone soft and seeking, as a genuine inquiry. "An ant can bite a human hard enough to catch the human's notice. Under some circumstances, they might even leave a mark that could be an irritant for a long time. If the human scratched it, maybe even a scar."

A little burst of air through Stanley's nostrils seemed like the start of a laugh, but then his eyes widened. "You're right."

"More often than not," she joked.

"What if the magic we used last time we were here left a mark on the creature? Something that was in no way truly lethal but an irritant of sorts. That could be why it stopped hunting for such a long time," Stanley said.

"That could also be why it's causing so much damage now. It's half-starved and angry."

He nodded, eyes unfocused as he sifted through his own thoughts.

"But what about Busar?" she asked.

Stanley's attention snapped back to her. "If some form of Busar is still alive, and he's out there and dangerous like you say, where is he? How does he fit into all this?"

"If the magic was strong enough to mark the monster, perhaps it was strong enough to mark the earth."

Burke poured the coffee and waited for Stanley to finish working out his thoughts. She'd seen him process ideas before. It was as if he had a team of file clerks in his brain. At moments, he'd send them all to work on a specific task, and to not disturb them, he'd sit still and quiet as a statue until they turned up with the useful tidbit he wanted.

"If that's true, that it marked the earth and something of that mark remains, and if we can figure out what it is, it might help us understand what effect it had on the creature," Stanley said.

Over the brim of her cup Burke said, "I have absolutely zero concept of what you mean."

"A magical scar, for lack of a better term, might be an energetic imbalance. It could leave a place wavering between this world and the next."

"Turn it into a spot where the veil is thin." She was catching on.

"Precisely, my dear." Stanley crossed his legs and tapped his chin with one finger—a sure sign he was urging the file clerks to work faster. "Powerful magic could also leave a physical scar. You've seen circles of unhallowed ground or blessed earth."

"Like Nathanial's house." She recalled visiting their friend in Santa Fe and finding daisies blooming amid a snowstorm.

Stanley beamed. His blue eyes twinkled. Stumbling on a clue always delighted him.

"Care to take a walk in the woods?" he asked.

"Oh, geez, Stanley. I was just looking out the window at the frozen gray landscape and thinking to myself that it seems like a perfect idea to go hiking in this God-awful weather."

He rose and clapped his hands together. "It's settled then. Have a seat. I'll fetch your boots and help you into them." Like a child going to the ice cream parlor, the old man practically skipped to her room and back.

Burke chugged the rest of her coffee. She needed a good

jolt of caffeine pumping through her blood. She let Stanley tuck her into waterproof, steel-toed boots and armed herself. Since becoming a hunter, only one time had she gone anywhere without her weapons. She was a quick learner. There wouldn't be a second time. She stuffed her right arm into her puffy winter coat sleeve, and Stanley zipped her up with her left arm still against her chest. It took an effort to ignore the empty sleeve flopping around, useless as a dead fish.

"Should we let Grandpa and Gordon know where we're going?" she asked.

Stanley pulled his phone from his pocket and dashed off a text. He started to put the phone away, hesitated, typed a second message, and then said, "Done. Ready?"

Sure. Raring to go.

He trotted to the cabin door and held it open for her. She stepped onto the creaking porch and heard him close and lock the door.

A blinging light swept over the porch, stealing away the entire world around Burke. A roar reminiscent of jet engines filled her ears, and though she never left the ground, she found her feet crashing back to earth. She stumbled forward, struggling to maintain her balance, her good arm flailing and smashing against something rough and unyielding. Stanley crashed into her back and knocked her into the tree she'd hit.

A tree?

On the porch?

She blinked rapidly to dispel the floating spots of light in her vision and took stock of their surroundings. On every side, moss-laden trees disappeared skyward into the unrelenting mist. The forest lay in unnatural silence before the birdsong and rustle of life slowly materialized. She wrapped the fingers of her right hand around the handle of her Sig Sauer and switched the safety off. Stanley held his weapon ready in a two-handed grip. He spun in a slow circle, eyes darting this way and that, taking in every detail.

Breathe. Inhale to a count of seven. Let it out just as slow.

Listen.

No human footsteps added an undernote to the symphony of wildlife, now once more in full bloom. They would have been unwelcome anyway given the circumstances, which had her hunter instincts on high alert. No sense warned her they were watched, or even that they were in immediate danger of any kind.

She lowered the gun. "What happened?"

A shake of the head was the only answer Stanley gave.

Burke traded her weapon for her phone. An annoying red line crossed the space where the signal bars should have been. "Do you have a signal?"

He checked and shook his head, but his attention was on a low, rocky hill thirty feet to the north. At least, Burke thought it was north. It was hard to tell, sheltered under the impenetrable canopy of leaves.

"I know this place," he murmured.

Her brows shot up. "Seriously? Where are we? How the hell did we get here?"

"We're in the forest."

Thank you, Captain Obvious. Burke bit her tongue and waited.

"This is southeast of the Makah Reservation. We must be twenty miles or more from the cabin."

"That's insane," she blurted. "How could that happen?"

He met her eyes. "Hunters are led to their hunt."

Not for the first time, Burke wondered if the fearless leader of their little team hadn't completely lost his mind. Then again, maybe she was the crazy one because when he started walking to what she thought was the east, she followed him even though that meant putting even more distance between them and the tiny remnants of civilization that existed in this lonely corner of the world.

CHAPTER ELEVEN

Richard

INSIDE THE COOL, STERILE MUNICIPAL BUILDING, A PIMPLY-faced kid with chocolate-brown eyes the size of tea saucers jumped out of his chair to greet Richard and Gordon. "You must be the feds." He held out a bony hand that engulfed Richard's when they shook. "Chief's expecting you."

Neither confirming nor denying the boy's assumption about their identity, they followed him to a tidy office with few decorations and a collection of books that left the thick wooden shelves bending under their weight. Chief Jason Harper stood to greet them. He was no more than five and a half feet tall, but what he lacked in height, he made up for in an impressive girth of ropy muscles. Even the hard lines of his face, framed in close-cropped, steel-colored fuzz, appeared to have been exercised and toned. When he moved, the seams of his clothing, stretched over his hulking form, defied the laws of physics by remaining intact.

"Gentlemen, sit, please." He nodded at the two chairs in front of his desk. "Your supervisor called and explained the purpose of your visit. I don't see how I can help, but I'll try. Damned shame what's happening to those kids."

Richard was impressed. With a voice like his, the policeman could have had a career singing bass with The Oak Ridge Boys. Or somebody more modern. Richard didn't keep up with new bands, but there were still some decent male quartets on the radio. Compared to the other two men in the room, his own voice was positively feminine. Maybe he ought to take some of that male enhancement stuff they were always advertising on television. He wouldn't mind a little testosterone boost that would give him muscles like the cop or a deep, powerful voice. It didn't seem shameful to admit that. What man couldn't use a bit of enhancing? He used to deny it, but he'd grown as a person in the last year.

"Richard?"

Richard blinked, recognized Gordon's voice, and remembered where he was.

Time to focus.

Dagnabbit, he'd already missed something. "What is it?"

Gordon searched Richard's face like he was trying to figure if he was having a stroke or something. "The chief had a question."

"Well, go on, then," he said to the pile of muscles in a uniform.

"It's just that your name seems familiar to me. I was thinking about it, and I seem to remember a Richard Bell being the father of one of my classmates back in Michigan. Madeline?"

Suspicion took a firm grip on Richard. He scowled. "You're yanking my chain."

"I assure you, I'm not. She worked on the newspaper, right? She was always doing stories about the wrestling team."

"I'll be dipped in bacon fat." He shook his head in amazement. "That's some kind of memory you got there. It's been a coon's age since Maddie graduated high school."

"I have a mind for names. It's been an asset over the years. I trust Madeline is well?"

"Turning into a regular world traveler these days," Richard said. "She's got a daughter of her own. The grandkid's as smart as a whip and goes at a fight, graceful and powerful as Ali."

Bushy brows raised over deep-set eyes raised a fraction of an inch. Probably, he didn't believe a girl could fight like that. Richard didn't judge the man. He'd operated under similar mistaken assumptions most of his life.

Gordon cleared his throat. "We don't want to take more of your time than we need to, Chief Harper. We're just trying to get a handle on what's happening with the little ones."

The man had a hard time tearing his eyes away from Richard to look at Gordon, but after an awkward moment, he gave a little shake like he was trying to clear his head. "The children, yes. Everyone's heard about it, of course, but they all seem to be natural deaths."

"But the ailment has not been diagnosed," Gordon said.

Harper shook his head. "No, sir. The medical examiner seemed just as stumped as everybody else. I pulled the reports if you'd like to take a look."

Gordon accepted a short stack of brown file folders and thanked the chief. Richard was impressed with the man. More often than not, they had to resort to threats or theft to lay hands on information like that. This guy was pleasantly helpful. A proper Midwest upbringing.

"Has anyone looked into environmental factors? Poison in the water? Air pollution? Mold, maybe?" Gordon asked.

A smirk spread on the chief's face. "Does this look like a part of the country where pollution is a major issue?"

Gordon stayed cool as a cucumber. "Eco-systems are interconnected. You could be breathing chemicals put into the air in

Seattle or eating fish poisoned by factories in Japan. All that aside, there are natural pollutants. In New England, there's a fungus that grows on corn. Ingested, it can cause hallucinations."

Harper grunted. "I'm sure the reports contain a complete list of the things the ME tested for. As far as I understand, everything came back clean."

"What about the families?" Richard asked.

"They're healthy, as far as I know," the chief said.

"But is there anything hinky?"

Gordon added to the question as if the man were a child who required clarification. "Abuse? Neglect?"

"Nothing like that. I know most of the folks up here. They're quiet people, just trying to make a living in the world. One of the families was off the grid, living in a camper on one of the forest trails."

"Ain't that illegal?" Richard asked.

The man shrugged. "Not my jurisdiction, and I'd be willing to admit those folks are cleaner and less disruptive to nature than any number of the tourists who go tromping through there getting themselves lost."

Richard considered the immensity of the forest and wondered how many people walked in and never came out again, on purpose or by accident. Most folks couldn't find their own butt with two hands, a flashlight, and a map, let alone navigate untouched wilderness successfully. In one sheepish corner of his mind, he admitted to himself that he was included in most people.

Gordon indicated the files. "We'd like to take these with us, compare them to our notes. We may speak with the families."

"You're welcome to the files. I'm sure I don't have to tell you those families have been through hell already. I'd ask you to do your damndest to make sure they aren't put in a position to relive that."

"There are kids sick in the hospital now, aren't there?" Gordon said.

The chief of police held Gordon's gaze for a long moment. "There are."

"We have no warrant, and I don't want to put you in an awkward position by asking anything further right now. We appreciate your time. You've been very helpful."

Richard was ready to go, his mind on dinner, but he did have one more question for the cop. "There was a guy outside. Looked about as old as Methuselah."

Chief Harper snorted. "That's Ray. I think he is as old as Methuselah. Ray's been an old man as far back as I can remember, and since your girl went to school with me, you know that's more than a New York minute."

"What's he do?" Richard asked.

The chief shrugged. "He does what old guys do. Sits on city benches and makes odd comments to passersby. Orders coffee from the diner and tips with coins. If he ever had a job, I don't know what it was. Local kids have all kinds of stories about him. He's a witch, a vampire, an alien from outer space." He shook his head. "So far as I've ever seen, he's just a lonely old man."

They shook hands all the way around, exchanged phone numbers, and then went back in the car.

"Well?" Gordon asked.

"It's getting late. Let's go back and eat dinner. We can ask more questions tomorrow, as if they're getting us anywhere."

This part of hunting was neither fun nor exciting. Half the time he didn't know what he was fishing for, and the other half he wondered if they were fishing in the right sea.

CHAPTER TWELVE

Burke

Since hunting with Stanley, Burke learned many things about supernatural creatures and human monsters. She'd learned new stories with roots deep in the soil of primeval humanity. She'd learned how to travel light, how to conceal a weapon on her body, and at countless roadside taverns, how to play a decent game of pool. She'd also learned that walking in a real forest was never straightforward.

Growing up in Michigan on the knife-edge between urban and rural, she'd heard stories of people lost in the woods. Search parties, often numbering near a hundred, would sometimes pass within feet of their quarry without spotting them. She'd rolled her eyes and muttered about how inept those seekers were.

Now, she understood. The forest stole the sky. Straight paths did not exist. At times, the undergrowth was so thick it was impenetrable, and if you were lucky enough to find a deer trail to save your legs from the inevitable scratches and bruises inflicted by crashing through the low plants and vines, you might end up going in a circle or arcing toward a hidden spot favored by the animals for reasons that didn't translate to human understanding. If there were hills, the body drifted downward under gravity's influence. Everything looked so alike the mind began asking if you'd already been to a spot. Probably you were just wandering deeper and deeper into the wilderness.

Before hunting, she'd seen the forest as just another landscape. Now she understood that a true, deep, old forest was a living thing that meant to draw in that which entered its heart and devour it.

She'd never been in a forest larger or older than this one.

The extraordinary canopy density meant the undergrowth was sparse enough to allow reasonably unrestricted movement. The biggest obstacle was the patches of ferns, each plant as large as a four-door sedan. She spotted scat from deer and bear, and once, in the distance, she was pretty sure she saw a moose.

Stanley moved at a steady, relentless trot. For reasons he'd never exactly explained, he'd managed to survive more than a hundred and forty years. A full century his junior, Burke found matching his stride to be a challenge despite regular runs on the treadmill.

She was thirsty, and cold and her shoulder throbbed in time with her pounding heart. The forest spooked her, and she didn't have the energy or patience to keep up the questioning that resulted in enigmatic half-answers. She simply plodded along behind Stanley, hoping he hadn't lost his marbles at last and led her to her death.

By the time they crested the rockiest, steepest hill they'd come to so far, the sparse sunlight that fought its way through the leaves and branches all but faded away. Burke pulled out her cell phone, useless for calling anyone from this lonely place but still functional as a bright flashlight. She stopped next to Stanley on the hilltop and moved the beam from left to right over the scene in front of them.

"What the...."

Every instinct screamed for her to draw her weapon, but to draw her weapon, she'd need to drop the light, and she did *not* want to be in the dark. The next time Nathanial made healing balm, she planned to take an extra portion to keep for herself for moments like this. Being one-armed drove her mad.

"I can't believe it," Stanley said. He stood, arms at his sides, not relaxed but not as anxious as the situation warranted. His revolver remained holstered. "I thought maybe it was so, but I can't believe it now that I see it with my own eyes."

Below them, a narrow valley had been gashed into the earth by some prehistoric titan force. The space was miraculously clear of trees, leaving a laceration in the rainforest's canopy through which the last weak rays of the day's light bled. Jagged rocks, covered in lush emerald-green moss, lined the sides of the valley, giving the impression the gorge was a mouth lined with teeth from which remnants of a green salad had not been properly scrubbed away.

The mouth chewed not salad, but bones, thousands upon thousands of them. Burke made out rib cages and femurs among countless smaller bits she couldn't identify. A myriad of skulls, ranging from no larger than a golf ball to much bigger than a human head, stared upward with hollow black eyes and rictus grins. Perhaps this is what the prophet, Ezekiel, saw when he wrote of the valley of dry bones. But these bones were not altogether dry. Bits of flesh, fur, and sinew remained, sending up an odor of rot that made her stomach roll.

To the left of where the hunters stood, as if stuck in one end of the depression like a plug, stood a massive rock outcropping with a near-perfect archway opening into the mass grave. Thick iron bars covered the opening. Mingled with the bones nearest the cave, metal tools reflected the spot of light shining from her phone.

"Do you know what's in there?" Burke asked.

Something rustled through the ferns on the opposite side of the gruesome scene.

Now, Stanley held his weapon at the ready.

A cougar, large and sleek as any lioness on the savannah, emerged from the growth. It watched them with wary yellow eyes for long, still moments. Apparently deciding they were no great threat, the cougar slunk to the far edge of the pile of bones and sniffed something that, from where Burke stood in the near darkness, looked like nothing more than a black lump. Whatever it was, the cat tore a piece away with a wet sound like breaking celery. Seconds later, she'd disappeared so completely Burke almost convinced herself she'd imagined the whole thing. Her attention returned to the crude rock and steel cage.

"Do you know what's in there?" she asked a second time.

Stanley lowered his gun to his side but did not holster the weapon. "I'm pretty sure it's Busar."

CHAPTER THIRTEEN

Richard

RICHARD TRIPPED OVER THE CABIN'S DOOR JAMB AND JUST about killed himself. How hard could it be to put a piece of yellow tape on the floor to remind a man there's a step there?

Nothing in the cabin appeared disturbed. Stanley's computer and a stack of familiar books of lore were piled on the small dining table, along with the leather-bound hunter's journal Stanley had inherited from Busar. A cup holding a half-inch of cold coffee rested on the counter next to the small coffee pot. No coats hung from the hooks near the door.

Richard shrugged. "Maybe they walked up to the main office to get some food."

"Maybe."

As if making its own suggestion, Gordon's phone chirped. Before he pulled the device from his pocket, Richard's phone buzzed like an angry wasp in his pocket. Both men consulted the tiny computers that demanded their attention.

"Coordinates?" Gordon asked.

Richard peered at the tiny screen through the bottom half of his progressive lenses.

47.62 124.349

"I reckon." He scowled. "Looks like Stanley sent this about 4:30. Why did it just now come through?" The clock above the cabin's kitchen sink read six p.m.

"Cell signals are a mess up here. It probably just caught a strong enough signal to get through." Gordon's thumbs dashed across the front of his phone while he spoke. "This isn't even two miles from here. We should go."

"Two miles which direction?"

"East, more or less."

Richard pushed his dentures around inside his mouth while he thought. "I ain't too sure a two-mile hike in the forest in the dark in wintertime is the brightest idea you ever had."

"What if they're in trouble?" Gordon asked.

"What if they're not, but we go out there and get mauled by a bear?" The skepticism grew in Gordon's eyes, and Richard held up a hand to stop any further discussion. "We done something like that once. Got our wires crossed, and everybody wasted a bunch of time looking for everybody else, running around like a bunch of chickens with our heads cut off. We made a two-hour rule."

Gordon raised a brow.

"Somebody says they'll be in a place at a time. They got two hours to show up before we send in the troops."

Both phones rang again. Both men looked at their new message.

Twenty-four hours.

"There you go," Richard said.

Gordon's head shook like he was an old man with palsy. "This isn't right. Twenty-four hours can be forever in a crisis situation. We can't just sit around waiting for them." He met Richard's gaze. "Aren't you worried about them?"

"I'm worried about them every darn day," Richard admitted. He clapped a hand on Gordon's shoulder. "There ain't two people in the world more likely to survive a night in the forest. They left here armed and dressed for the weather. Whatever they were doing, they had a plan."

"And that plan included asking us to wait twenty-four hours before we go after them?"

Richard nodded. He felt for Burke's guy. The waiting was the hardest part, and Gordon had been a man of action his whole life. "We got work of our own to do." No better tonic for nerves existed than staying busy. "We ought to round up some grub. Can't get nothing done on an empty stomach."

"All right," Gordon agreed. "We can go over these files while we eat and make a plan for tomorrow."

Richard went to the fridge and tugged on the handle. Burke had picked up a sack full of groceries at some place back in Colorado. Inside the refrigerator, he found a package of turkey bologna, a loaf of whole-grain bread, and a disposable pan full of sushi.

He slammed the door shut. "Ain't nothing here a man can eat."

"Hmm?" "Gordon sat at the table, rifling through the files.

"We passed a restaurant on the way in. Can't be more than a mile or so south of here."

"Sure. Okay." He snapped the folder shut, scooped up the stack of files, and led the way back out of the cabin.

Richard was about to step from the small porch onto the first step when a dark blob near the base of the railing caught his eye. He squatted to inspect the object, and both knees popped like Fourth of July firecrackers. At first glance, he'd thought the object was some kind of small black animal. It looked furry but, close up, it obviously wasn't alive. It looked more like a rock, slightly smaller than his fist, covered in a tight velvet wrapping. It sat in the center of a perfect circle that had burned into the weather-treated planks.

"What is that?" Gordon asked.

Richard scanned the ground and spotted a pine twig. "Hand me that twig."

Gordon did. Richard poked it with the twig, and the mysterious object disintegrated into ash.

"Some kid burning stuff out here?" Gordon asked. "Maybe the last people who stayed in the cabin? It's weird looking."

"Queer as a three-dollar bill," Richard agreed.

Vague uneasiness plagued him. He pushed his dentures around his mouth while he thought about it. His stomach growled. He'd seen something like this before, but it wasn't the same. Different size. Different shape. Different circumstances. Best to keep his thoughts to himself for the time being. He didn't need to shoot off his trap every time some half-baked idea popped into his mind. If empty wagons made the most noise, the smart thing was to sometimes keep your trap shut.

Rising to his full height again required both hands on the railing and a groan loud as an elephant fart. "I'll think about it while we eat. Protein makes a man's brain work better."

Gordon neither argued nor commented. He was a quiet guy. In Richard's book, that's a checkmark in the plus column.

They found the restaurant parking lot to be nearly deserted.

"How come nobody's eating here?" Richard asked as Gordon pulled into a spot beside the diner. "It's prime dinnertime."

"The guy that rented us the cabin said nobody comes here this time of year."

"Don't blame them. This damp air is colder than a pocket full of penguin poop. It gets inside your bones." He climbed out into the frigid night and looked up at the rough-hewn archway of the restaurant. "This place looks promising, though. Bet they've got something in there that'll stick to a man's ribs and warm him up."

Gusty swirls of warm air pulled them inward when Gordon opened the door. A girl an inch or two taller than Richard stood next to the hostess station. She had a jet-black braid that hung over her shoulder almost to her waist, a round face with dark, tilted eyes and full lips that she'd painted bright pink. Her white sweater stretched across bosoms that defied gravity, and her short skirt gave a glimpse of legs that went on for about a mile.

"Good evening, gentlemen. Table for two?"

"Unless you'd care to join us," Richard said.

She smiled, and the room grew a little warmer.

"I knew right away, just from looking at the way this place was built, it was going to be good," he told her.

"I hope we can exceed your expectations." She grabbed two menus and two sets of silverware wrapped in black cloth napkins from a nearby table, then led them to a table near a window that looked out over a wide river rushing toward the ocean and offered her hopes that they'd enjoy their meal.

Right away, Gordon had his nose back in the files.

"What are you looking for, exactly?" Richard asked.

"Anything that says these deaths aren't natural. Anything that connects the families. Maybe they've all visited the same restaurant or hiked the same trails."

"You ain't going to find that in the ME's report."

"Probably not," Gordon agreed.

With a shrug, Richard opened his menu. He scanned the appetizers for one of those big fried onion flowers with the spicy dip. That would surely go a long way toward warming him up from the inside out.

Spinach artichoke dip.

Korean salmon rillette.

Oysters on the half-shell.

Bah! Who ate crap like that? Who even knew what any of

that was? Burke would know, but she would never convince him to eat it. He skipped over *Salads and Greens* and moved on to *Land and Sea*.

Dungeness crab mac and Beecher's cheese. Twenty-seven dollars.

"They got thirty-dollar mac and cheese on this menu," he told Gordon, who still hadn't taken a look.

Gordon grunted.

What was that supposed to mean?

"Nearly thirty dollars for mac and cheese. Who's going to pay that much, even if they have it? Do they know you can buy a box of mac and cheese at the discount grocery for twenty-nine cents?"

"Get it if you want it," Gordon said. "You have to get something."

"I don't want it for thirty dollars. And it's got fish in it. What kind of a weirdo puts fish in macaroni?"

Gordon's eyes moved left to right over the pages in front of him. Richard harrumphed and returned to his menu, still holding out hope for a reasonable meal.

Crispy salmon katsu.

Braised stuffed eggplant.

Vegan burger.

Southern chicken cassoulet.

A kid with blonde curls hanging in his watery blue eyes loped up the table on skinny legs, long as stilts. "Have we decided what we'd like?"

"I ain't decided. This menu's weird. You got a plain old burger?"

"We have a delightful vegan burger. It's very popular among our regular visitors."

Richard harrumphed. "If it's vegan, then, by definition, it ain't a burger."

"We have an elk burger that comes with pickled onions."

Richard rolled his eyes.

The kid fidgeted with the black order book in his bony hands. "We have a ribeye steak, served smothered in port-stewed shallots and blue cheese butter."

"How much is that?"

"Fifty-seven dollars."

"For one steak? I can buy a steak at the Walmart for six bucks."

The waiter chewed his lip. Richard wondered if the kid would burst into tears. He sighed and handed over the ridiculous menu. A man had to eat something, and these folks here seemed to know that people in that area didn't have many options.

"Give me the steak. Don't smother it in anything that didn't come out of the salt and pepper shakers. It comes with fries or something?" He was still holding out hope.

"Roasted garlic mashed potatoes."

It wasn't perfect, but it was better than a poke in the eye with a sharp stick. "Fine."

Looking as relieved as a man pardoned from execution, the kid turned to Gordon. "And for you, sir?"

"Uhm, I'll have the burger," he said without looking up.

"With everything on it?"

"Sure."

Quick as a whip, the kid turned and high-tailed it out of there.

"Just about the stupidest menu I ever saw," Richard said.

"Doesn't seem much different from what we had back on the cruise ship."

Richard remembered the stupid food they'd been served each night on the cruise. There was a lot to be said for the buffet and the room service, but the dinners were like some kind of practical joke.

"What do you see in those files?"

Still not looking up, Gordon just shook his head. "Not a damned thing. With the deaths ruled as natural, nobody gathered much information. The autopsies confirmed what the doctors said. They just got weak. Their organs failed, and they died. No viral infections, no parasites, no identifiable poison."

Near the front door, a woman raised a ruckus, yelling at the pretty young hostess and gesturing wildly. Richard tried to ignore her and focus on the case.

"No bruises? Bites? Signs of trauma?"

"Nothing," Gordon said. "One kid had a healed fracture in his—"

Frantic words cut through the air. "All I want to know is who was driving that car."

Both men looked toward the woman. Her eyes locked on Richard's, and she stormed across the room like five feet six inches of gray-haired fury. A puffy red coat with a high-necked shirt poking up above the collar hid her top half, but her bottom half was encased in tight jeans that showed she still had all the sweet curves God gave her, even if she'd also acquired crow's feet and the tiniest hint of a waddle under her chin. The thin, angry slash of her mouth was painted red, and she'd taken the time to doll up her bright green eyes.

She halted at their table. "Is that your convertible?"

"If you mean the Cadillac, it belongs to a friend of ours," Gordon said.

She pressed a hand to her heart and swayed like a birch sapling in a tornado.

The hostess caught up, tottering on her spikey-heeled shoes. "I'm so sorry."

Gordon waved her away. "It's okay." He gestured to one of the empty chairs at the table, "Please, sit."

The woman sat, and the hostess wandered away as if unsure that was the right thing to do.

"What's got your goose?" Richard asked the old lady. All the blood had drained from her face, and a thin line of sweat broke out across her upper lip. "You ain't having a heart attack or something, are you?"

She blinked and looked at him again, frowning as if confused by his question. "A heart attack?" After taking a moment to consider, she shook her head. "No. No, I'm fine. I just...." She scanned the restaurant, taking extra time to examine the other three tables where people had returned their attention from her to their own business. "Is that... I mean.... Are you...? Stanley Kapcheck is back."

Richard rolled his eyes.

"You know Stanley?" Gordon asked.

All the color that had drained out of her cheeks and a good bit more flooded into her face, leaving her pink as a rose. "Yes. I knew him."

Biblically, Richard thought. *Friggin' Stan Kapcheck.*

"He's alive?" she asked.

"Yes," Gordon said.

Good old Gordon, a man of few words.

She looked around again.

Richard wondered if she thought the old fart was hiding under the table, or something. He ought to spare her the drama. "He ain't here with us."

While she considered what to say next, the two men exchanged a clueless glance. Who could understand what was going on in a woman's brain? There was a time he'd have asked what she was thinking, but he'd learned that wasn't often a good idea either. Best to wait it out and see where she led.

Before she said anything else, the string bean of a waiter showed up with two bowls of salad. Who asked for rabbit food? Not Richard. He knew that much.

"Why don't you order something," Gordon suggested to the stranger who'd taken up residence at their table.

She nodded. "Yes. That's a good idea. Gin and tonic, please."

After the kid slumped off toward the kitchen, she shucked her coat. Turned out the top half was just as curvy as the bottom half. Richard couldn't fault Stanley's taste.

"Stanley Kapcheck was here over thirty years ago," she told them.

That added up to what they already knew. If this woman was in her sixties now, she would have been ripe as a peach thirty years ago. And Stanley would have been somewhere about a hundred and ten years old.

Richard grimaced.

"I never thought he'd come back. When he disappeared, he was so completely gone. I hired detectives, and the stories they came back with." A girlish giggle bubbled out of her, and she relaxed against the back of the chair. The smile took her beauty from notable to breathtaking.

"Why did you want to find him so badly?" Gordon asked.

Before she could answer, the lanky waiter showed up and plopped her cocktail on the table. "Food'll be out in a minute."

Usually, the one upside of a menu full of stuff nobody had ever heard of was that the service was good. Richard was hard-pressed to figure out why they were paying a hundred bucks to eat there. Tomorrow, he'd just get some sandwich fixings or bring a pizza back from Port Angeles.

"Does anyone else know that Stanley's back?" the woman asked.

Her failure to answer Gordon's question caught Richard's attention.

"We've only arrived in the area today," Gordon answered, equally vague.

She guzzled half the gin in one go and dropped the glass on the tabletop with a thunk.

Gordon jabbed his fork into his salad. "What's your name?"

"What?" She seemed startled by the question. "Oh, I'm

sorry. I just...the shock of seeing that car sent me into a flutter. I'm Loretta Youngblood."

Loretta. Of course, she was a Loretta.

"My name is Gordon. This is Richard. We're friends of Stanley's."

Lovey Loretta propped her forearms on the table and leaned on them, holding her cocktail glass between her palms. She spoke in a near whisper. "Are you heroning, hun?"

"What?" Richard asked. He fiddled with his hearing aid, and it squealed. "Speak up."

"Why would you ask that?" Gordon asked.

What had she asked? What the heck was heroning?

"I know what Stanley does." Again, with the furtive glances, as if anybody cared what they were talking about. "He helped me once."

Her words became clear like the tumblers of a lock clicking into place. Not heroning hunt, but here on a hunt. Yes, that made more sense.

With one finger, tipped in crimson nail polish, she tugged on the collar of her sweater, revealing a jagged, twisting scar along the side of her neck. "I had no idea that vampires.... I mean, how could I? Who thinks any of that is real?" She let go of her collar and finished her cocktail. "Thank God he was here. I don't even think he came just to get rid of them, but he never told me the real answer, probably because the other guy didn't want me to know. That guy was cagey. He didn't seem to trust anyone."

"The other guy?" Gordon asked.

Loretta nodded. "Tall Black fellow. I don't know what happened between the two of them, but it surprised me he stayed behind when Stanley left."

Gordon pushed his food to the side. "What makes you think Busar stayed behind?"

"Well, it was no big secret. He'd be at the grocery. Sometimes I saw him at the Sinclair station, back before it burned down. Not often, but now and then, I'd bump into him."

Richard peeked at the kitchen door. That steak would be welcome on the table any time now. "You see him recently?"

Her answer came without hesitation. "Recently? No." She lifted her glass to drink, realized it was empty, and lowered it back to the table. "I can't remember the last time. It's been quite a while."

"A year?" Gordon asked.

"More like ten, maybe fifteen."

Lanky McRudewaiter slammed through the kitchen door, balancing a large tray on his long, twiggy arms. Richard's mouth watered while he waited for the meat and potatoes to be delivered. It was overpriced, but he was so hungry he'd have paid twice as much for a meal.

Gordon was like a dog with a bone on the subject of Busar. "Where did he go, ten or fifteen years ago?"

"How should I know?" Loretta asked. "I bumped into him now and then, and then I didn't."

"Did he have ties in the community?"

"Not that I'm aware of." She leaned to the side to allow the waiter to set their plates down and asked for a refill on her drink. "Does he have something to do with your hunt? You never did tell me if Stanley is with you."

"We'd like to find Busar," Gordon said. "To be entirely honest, we're not sure what we're looking at up here if anything. People die. It's not always the work of monsters."

"I need to know if Stanley Kapcheck is here," she insisted.

"Why?" Richard asked.

Loretta's pretty green eyes flashed like lightning. Energy buzzed and crackled along her fingertips. Both men scooted back. Gordon's right hand dropped out of sight, and Richard would have bet his fingers were wrapped around the handle of his Smith and Wesson.

She took a shaky breath, and her own personal little thunderstorm receded. "Is Stanley here?"

"We don't know where he is." Technically, Gordon was telling the truth, but it was a pretty fine line.

After holding Gordon's gaze for a long enough time that it set Richard's nerves on edge, she rose. "When you speak with Stanley, please tell him that I would very much like to speak with him. He'll know where to find me." Loretta gathered her coat and sashayed out of the restaurant as abruptly as she'd entered. She looked just as good going out as she had coming in.

"What the hell was that?" Gordon asked.

Richard shook his head and cut into his steak. "Who knows?"

Friggin' Stan Kapcheck.

CHAPTER FOURTEEN

Burke

Stanley and Burke picked their way along the edge of the pile of bones. Stanley rustled through the debris, making no effort to be stealthy while Burke placed each foot with care, cringing at the snap of bone beneath her weight.

By the time they reached the mouth of the cave with its three-inch steel bars, no remnant of light remained. Velvety blackness stretched above them, removing the sky and leaving only an abyss uninterrupted by even a pinpoint of starshine.

The sensation that everything in this place was bigger, older, more powerful, and more malevolent than the world around it unsettled Burke. She followed the light from the phone Stanley held in his left hand. In his right hand, he gripped his revolver. Burke held her own weapon at the ready. Whether a monster in the cave or a more natural predator sneaking up from behind, she was loathe to be left defenseless.

Ten feet separated them from the mouth of the cave.

"Leave," a low voice commanded.

So brief was the moment of Stanley's hesitation Burke thought she might have imagined it.

"I will not leave," Stanley said.

In the unnaturally white light from the phone, two dark hands with stained, chipped, yellowing nails at the end of the long, thick fingers wrapped around the bars. Low laughter rolled out of the cave-like distant thunder.

"You will not leave? But why not? That's what you do, isn't it?"

If she strained, Burke could make out the whites of two eyes in the darkness.

Six feet away now.

"I stay as long as I must. I leave when it is the only remaining action," Stanley replied.

"Is that what you tell yourself so you can sleep soundly at night? You tell yourself you had no choice? There was nothing left for you to do?"

Three feet away, a figure drew to a stop. Stanley held the phone at a low angle, so the harshest part of the light struck the man's broad, powerful chest and cast long shadows over his sharp-featured face. Busar's arms were thick as Burke's legs. His thighs resembled tree trunks. He stood before them, naked and shameless.

"A hunter always has one more trick to play, Stanley. At least, any decent hunter. I thought you were a decent hunter. I was wrong."

The urge to defend Stanley exploded within Burke like an erupting volcano. "Stanley is the best hunter in the world. He's saved more lives than anyone will ever know."

Busar's gaze shifted to her, silencing her. Surely, he could see her heart; he knew her deepest thoughts and could cast the steel bars aside with ease and tear her limb from limb.

"Put your gun away, girl. You've not come all this way to

shoot me. Tell me, has Stanley finally committed to a single lover?"

"Burke is my partner and more naturally capable than anyone I've ever known. She is not my lover."

"More like a daughter, perhaps?"

"A fair statement," Stanley said.

"Then I urge caution, lest she witness the destruction of your soul and abandon you to face endless torment alone."

"No decent parent would ask their child to stand by their side while they descended into madness," Stanley replied.

Busar's eyes narrowed. "You are as petulant and selfish as you've ever been."

"And you still command on high as though you believe yourself one of the gods."

Sudden, semi-hysterical laughter took hold of Burke. These two old men, one of them naked as Adam, were seriously going to stand in the middle of the forest, in the middle of the night, bickering and trading insults? Busar laughed, too, and for reasons she wouldn't be able to explain if she lived another hundred years, that struck her as even funnier.

Once the laughter died, Busar spoke again, his voice still full of the booming laughter that shook him moments earlier. "I am one of the gods, now, Stanley. Shall we call it self-fulfilling prophecy?" With one enormous hand, he gestured to the valley behind them. "I am the god of death. These creatures understood that. They came to me to sacrifice themselves upon my altar." Again, he held the bars and moved even closer. "Is that why you've come, Stanley? Unable to do anything useful, as a form of penance for your innumerable sins, have you come to offer your life in sacrifice?"

Stanley stood, feet planted, back straight, shoulders square, unyielding as stone. "Are you killing children?"

Busar's laughter filled the night again, the sound of a jolly

Santa Claus, driven mad by his inner demons. "I am prisoner in this cage, am I not?"

"Tell me how you came to be here, like this. When I left...."

His words trailed away, giving Burke no further insight into the situation when Stanley saw fit to leave his mentor behind.

When Busar backed away from the mouth of the cave, it was as if he merged into the darkness. Only his eyes remained visible, reflecting the light from Stanley's phone. He moved closer to the earth, and Burke surmised he had sat down.

"I tried, Stanley, to live a normal life. I walked among them, careful in every action to bring no harm, but you know what happened, don't you?"

"Your existence is an imbalance. Everything that came near you spiraled into chaos."

"I am the god of death," Busar repeated.

Burke shivered, despite her warm layers.

"To live among men meant their destruction," Busar said. "You and I knew this place to be safe from prying eyes. No one comes to this part of the forest, thanks to the dryads' warding."

"You caged yourself." Stanley's words were carried on an exhale. At last, his shoulders dropped a fraction. He shook his head. "How long?"

"I have been in this place for four thousand five hundred and four days. I have been alone, starving, witnessing the death of every creature that dared come close, every plant that dared take root near me, and now you are here, Stanley, my pupil, my son, and you have brought your own protégé. You will both die. Whatever is killing children will go on killing. The children will die. Earth will go on and on, and everything will die, and still I will sit in this cave, forgotten by men and monsters. I will not die."

Silence prowled through the valley. No insects buzzed. No owl called out in the night. Just the thumping of Burke's own heartbeat.

"We need to save the children." She winced at the volume of her own voice, a thunderbolt in the stillness.

"Why?" Busar asked.

"Because we are hunters. We were led here."

"Were you? Led by whom?"

"On a hunt in Santa Fe, we came across Christine." Stanley's voice remained cool and steady as ever.

Nothing moved. No breath of wind stirred. Beyond the small circle of light, the world ceased to exist.

"She is well, grown now, a doctor," he continued.

"How nice for her," Busar said.

"It was time for me to return. I knew that children were dying, and then Christine was sent to me."

"By God. Is that what you believe?"

"You know it is."

Busar laughed and approached the bars again. "Hunters are led to their hunts by a benevolent overseer who uses them to save lives?"

"That is what you taught me."

"And after saving hundreds of lives, thousands, God will let the monsters kill you. Or, perhaps, if God feels a special kind of hatred toward you, you'll be turned into something like this." He indicated his own filthy body.

"God does not hate," Stanley said.

"Truly? You say that to me? If God does not hate, why have I been left in this torment after playing my part in His Grand Game for so many, many years?"

Stanley shook his head, as though he were sorting through arguments internally and rejecting them one by one.

An idea, stunning in its absurdity but certainly accurate, bloomed in Burke's mind as she listened to the two men argue the nature of the world. "You are here because this is your hunt. We need you."

His teeth, bared in a wide grin, gleamed in the darkness. "This one is something else. Where did you find her?"

Stanley holstered his gun. He'd decided there was no threat, the gun wouldn't help him face the threat, or maybe he'd gotten tired of holding it. It was hard to tell with Stanley sometimes.

"I broke my leg during a hunt. The Devil stole my car. I was hurt and needed a ride, and she helped me."

Busar's attention returned to Burke. "Why did you help him?"

A small spark of her earlier amusement was reborn as she considered her answer. Anyone except a seasoned hunter would have had many other questions to ask after hearing a tale like the one Stanley just told.

She didn't want to lie, but if Stanley kept Richard's existence under wraps, there must be a reason. This encounter felt like being tested by a dangerous mystic on a mountaintop. Each word carried vital weight, and a wrong choice could crush them all. "It seemed like the right thing, and I didn't have anything else to do."

"You are bold," Busar said.

"Thank you," Burke replied.

"Even if I wanted to—and I don't, especially—I can't help you." He tugged on the bars. Muscles rippled beneath his smooth skin. "I was careful in my design. I am trapped in here until the earth falls down around me."

"We will get you out," Stanley said.

"I doubt that, but if you do, the blood of those who die because of my freedom is on your hands."

The two men stared at one another, neither speaking nor moving for a full minute. Burke put her gun in the pocket of her coat. The gun wouldn't help her if he decided to attack, and quite frankly, she was tired of holding it.

"We'll return in the morning," Stanley said.

"Don't," Busar said.

Stanley turned away and started climbing the hill, moving away from the carnage across the valley floor. Burke followed in silence.

He spoke without looking back. "I must."

CHAPTER FIFTEEN

Richard

Morning didn't dawn over the remote cliffside where the cabin sat. It crept up and peeked shyly over the eastern horizon, shedding watery gray light that allowed a person to see but failed to bring out the colors of the world. Looking out the window was like peering into a washed-out black-and-white photograph.

Richard sat on the edge of the squeaky bed and watched gulls swirling over the sea in lazy circles. Anxiety gnawed at his gut. He'd dismissed Gordon's concerns about Burke and Stanley the night before because if he got to chewing that bone, he'd never be able to let it go.

What the heck were they doing out in the middle of the forest?

How did they get there?

Burke hadn't taken her medication with her. What if she was in pain?

The twenty-four hours Stanley had asked for wouldn't be up

until evening. The other end of the day seemed as far away as the other end of the universe. Couldn't Stanley have written a note on paper like any reasonable human would have done?

Friggin' Stan Kapcheck.

Like two shots from a double-barrel shotgun, Richard's knees popped when he stood up. He hitched along a few steps until his tinker-toy hip kicked into full gear. By the time he showered and dressed in a warm jogging suit, Gordon was at the kitchen table, his white notecards spread in front of him. He shuffled them, scanned the new order, and reshuffled them.

"What's that?" Richard poured water in the tiny coffee pot and peeled the lid off the can of fresh ground dark roast. Kudos to Burke. She always bought the good coffee. Gone were his days of gulping down bitter instant brew.

"It's how I think." He slid one of the cards from the middle to the end of the row. "I've found that the brain tends to process information in the order it's received. If I break it into pieces and rearrange it, sometimes I can see new patterns and connections."

"Is it working?"

Gordon slumped back against his chair and sipped his coffee. "It's like trying to figure out the picture on a five-hundred-piece puzzle when you've only got ten pieces." He set the heavy mug aside, then tapped the card in the upper left-hand corner with one stubby-nailed finger. "At least two of the kids went to the same doctor."

His hand moved over five cards in a neat row. "We got five kids so far. Those are the five we know of. There could be more. People in a remote place like this are probably used to doing things their own way at home." The next card had Loretta's name written on it. Next to Loretta was the guy outside the police station. "Stanley is remembered here."

Richard harrumphed. He took his cup from the coffee maker and eased himself into the chair next to Gordon.

"Tell me," Gordon said. "Am I correct in assuming that, when you arrive in a town, you get in, do the job as quickly as possible, and get out again with as little fuss as possible?"

"That's generally the plan, yeah."

"You keep a low profile, right?"

Hot coffee settled in Richard's belly, warming him up from the inside out. "We try. Sometimes it's easier said than done."

"Okay, but it's been, what? Thirty years since Stanley was up here? Why do people still remember him? Whatever he had with Loretta, it was more than a one-night stand that happened back when George Bush was president."

There was no arguing with that. Whatever Stanley had done to the woman, she was still in a right tizzy over it.

Gordon crossed his arms and scowled. "What was she, anyway?"

Richard knew what he meant. The woman was literally electric. "Ain't like nothing I ever saw before. Stan did say there was a whole heap of monsters in these woods, though."

"It's not hard to believe," Gordon said.

The two of them sipped their coffee and stared at the minuscule collection of information. Gordon was the first to speak. "I'm not comfortable pretending like it's fine and normal that Burke and Stanley disappeared into the forest last night."

"Me either," Richard said.

"But you don't think we should go look for them, do you?"

"Stan said twenty-four hours. There must have been a reason."

The second hand completed its cycle on the clock above the kitchen window.

"Do you think that people remembering Stanley has anything to do with what's happening to those kids? Are we solving more than one mystery?" Gordon asked.

"I seen some stuff that would put hair on your mama's chest and make it curly, but I ain't got more idea of what's going on up here than Adam. I keep thinking, if it is this so-called boogeyman, what then? If Stanley couldn't kill it the first time, what makes us any more able to kill it now?"

With an immense sigh, Gordon scooped the cards into a pile and tucked them into the front cover of Stanley's hunter's journal. "Let's drive up to Port Angeles and see what we can learn from the ME up there. When we get back, if they're not here, we'll go find them."

Lacking any better plan, Richard nodded, but he didn't get up. "Did we ever tell you about the first big hunt the three of us did together?"

"Not that I recall."

Feelings of terror, confusion, deep grief, and immense satisfaction wove through the tapestry of that story. Richard tried to see past all that. "It was a skinwalker."

"Is that like a shapeshifter?" The ease with which Gordon was assimilating information about monsters had earned Richard's admiration. Neither he nor Burke took to the idea of supernatural creatures living amongst them with such grace.

"Shapeshifter can change into darn-near anything. Skinwalker changes into different people. Sounds kind of like this boogeyman, though. It drains a person's life away until they just wither up and die."

Gordon's brows angled sharply over his eyes. "You're thinking that's what this is?"

Not exactly. Stanley had said it was different. Who was he to argue? Relatively speaking, he was still brand new. Richard sighed. "I'm just keeping an open mind."

Compared to Forks, Port Angeles was downright metropolitan. Small houses with scrubby yards lined wide streets. Familiar fast-food restaurants and chain stores squatted on busy street corners. Here, where occasional average-sized trees and scrappy weeds were the primary signs of vegetation, bright winter sun burned away the mist.

Gordon parked the Cadillac in one of only a handful of remaining spots in the large lot next to the orange and white building that housed the medical examiner's office. Rather than exiting the vehicle, he sat with his hands on the steering wheel, one finger tapping a cadence against the leather cover.

"You're still worried about them?" Richard guessed.

"I'm having trouble thinking of anything else."

"Stanley left us a job to do. We need to do it."

The weight of Gordon's gaze fell on Richard. "Do you honestly accept everything Stanley says at face value?"

Richard never gave the matter much thought. He scratched his scalp and felt the hairs jump up in the wake of his fingers. There'd be no hope in getting them to lay down again now, but he patted them in a vain attempt anyway.

"Stanley Kapcheck is a prancing old fool, makes me crazy more often than not. But when it comes to this business of hunting monsters, I trust him like I ain't never trusted anybody in my whole life. The stuff I've seen him do..." he shook his head, lacking the words to describe the feats of strength and cunning he'd witnessed. "Don't matter if he tells me the whole story. He's pulled my bacon out of the fire more often than I can say. If he tells me something, it's what I need to know."

"I hate not knowing everything. I've hated it my whole life. I went into this line of work because I liked being the guy who filled in the blanks."

After chewing on that, Richard said, "That's what we're doing, isn't it? Let's go inside and fill in the blanks. You get enough of those little white cards, maybe they'll start to look like something." He reached for the door handle. "Besides, it'll make you crazy to sit around worrying like an old woman. Better to be in motion."

They passed rows full of pickup trucks and four-door sedans that bore the scars of a decade or more of daily use. A single snazzy black convertible stuck out like a sore thumb in the middle of the sea of working-class vehicles. Maybe that's why everyone around these parts noticed the Cadillac. They didn't see many fancy cars, so they tended to catch the eye.

A receptionist greeted them in a voice as cool as the rolling gray waters of the northern Pacific. Her black hair was pulled back in a bun so tight it pulled the corners of her eyes upward. "You're expected. Come with me." She rose.

The men exchanged a glance, then followed her down a hallway to an elevator.

"The ME works in the basement," she explained.

"I can't imagine there is a lot of forensic work to be done in this part of the country," Gordon said.

The woman never flinched a muscle or batted an eyelash. The animatronic figures at a kids' pizza place had more personality. "There isn't a lot of murder here if that's what you mean. But anywhere humans live there are unexplained deaths—sudden onset illnesses, accidental poisonings, attacks—animal attacks, I mean. We've seen more than a few logging accidents over the years."

"What kind of animals would attack a human around here?" Gordan asked.

"The list of animals that wouldn't attack a human around here would be shorter," she said.

A sharp bell signaled their arrival at the lowest level of the building, and the men followed their guide through yet more halls. The white walls reflected the bland light emanating from the humming fluorescent bulbs, sanitizing any pretense of warmth or comfort from the space. The echoes of their footsteps chased after them as they walked. Richard couldn't resist the urge to peek over his shoulder and make sure no one followed.

On the wall beside a Dutch door, the top half of which stood open, a little wooden-veneer plaque read *County Morgue*. A clipboard bearing a rumpled sheet of paper leaned on the ledge at the top of the lower half of the door. Across the top someone wrote *PLEASE SIGN IN* with a black marker.

Gordon scrawled an illegible signature across one of the lines and handed the pen to Richard.

"I'll leave you to it, then," the receptionist said. When she walked away, her heels clicked like ice cubes against glass.

Richard signed his name before taking a moment to glance around the interior of the office. He found the vast difference between the two sides of the doors as disorienting as staring into another dimension. A worn Oriental carpet covered the industrial flooring. In lieu of harsh overhead lighting, four floor lamps offered warm illumination. Vases full of flowers filled nooks between rows of books on shelves that lined the walls. Tarnished silver frames surrounded photographs that ranged from sepia prints of stern-looking folks in heavily starched Victorian garb to high-definition snapshots of sunsets over the sea.

Amid the shabby opulence, a sturdy wooden desk faced two squashy-looking armchairs with an upholstered ottoman situated so that a person in either seat could rest their feet.

A man with a pair of cheap black oxfords with scuffed-up toes propped his legs on the footstool. The gentleman crossed his ankles, his brown slacks hiked up far enough to reveal black socks with neon green aliens printed on them.

"Come in, gentlemen," he said without attempting to rise and greet them.

Gordon turned the handle, and the bottom half of the door opened with a squeak that made Richard wince. Even the smell inside the office differed from the institutional odor of the rest of the building. This room reminded Richard of the scent of the fancy soap and candle stores Burke favored. He rubbed his tickling nose and crossed the carpet a step behind Gordon.

"Thank you for taking the time to see us today," Gordon said.

At last, Richard could see the guy in the chair. The Clallam County medical examiner laid the book he was reading in his lap and gazed up at them with obsidian eyes that had no whites. His pale skin glowed in the soft lamplight as if it had a luminescence all its own. When he smiled, the points of two sharp fangs glistened.

"I'm a humble servant of the people. How may I help you?"

Richard pointed his gun at the guy before he had time to think about whether or not he should take it out. "What are you doing here, ghoul?"

The monster in the chair cocked his head. "This is my office, hunter. Are you going to shoot me? It won't hurt me, but it will do terrible things to this shirt, and it's only a few weeks old."

"Richard?" Gordon held his gun in both hands. "What the hell, man?" Gordon's words came out smooth and calm. He wasn't a guy who panicked in the heat of the moment. It was almost like Burke stumbled upon the male version of herself. Did that make their relationship something weird?

Richard blinked. *Focus, man.*

"He's a ghoul. They eat the flesh of the dead."

"Precisely. The dead. Not the living. So, you can't possibly have a thing to fear from me," the ghoul said. "Why not lower the weapons so that we can have a civilized conversation?"

"Ghouls can change people," Richard warned Gordon.

His finger itched on the trigger, but the thing was right. He was packing regular old ammo from the sporting goods store. It wouldn't even leave a bruise.

The medical examiner sighed deeply and closed his book.

"Enough of this nonsense. Why in the world would I want to change you?" He held his hands out, palms up. "I want to help you. Sit, please."

Gordon holstered his weapon but remained standing beside Richard.

"Perhaps I went about this in the wrong way. My intention was to be honest with you, not to frighten you."

"I ain't scared," Richard protested. It would have been more convincing if his voice didn't squeak like a mouse at the end of the statement.

"Good." The monster lowered his feet to the floor and leaned forward to set his book on the edge of the desk. "I am Dr. Harold Lewis, Clallam County Medical Examiner, and I believe we have something to talk about."

"If hunters are led to their hunts, maybe we were led here to hunt you," Gordon said.

It seemed like solid logic.

"Maybe you were," the gruesome doctor said. "But you should hold off until we've spoken about the real reason you came here."

Gordon folded his arms across his chest. "How is it that you came to be employed by the county?"

The ghoul raised one brow. "I worked hard. I went to medical school." He rose and circled around to the other side of the desk. He produced a pair of dark glasses and a set of prosthetic teeth from a drawer. Now he resembled a blind man with a sunscreen addiction. "Surely, you've learned that we 'monsters' have found ways to move among the humans."

"And now you've got the best job in the world. You get to work down here in the dark, and every time a new body comes in, the buffet is open."

Dr. Lewis took a seat behind the desk and folded his hands on top of the large calendar that covered most of the surface. "It's the circle of life. I don't hurt anyone. Sit," he said again.

"Let us solve the mystery of the dying children. That is why you're here, isn't it?"

Two voices in Richard's mind played tug of war.

Hunters, by definition, are supposed to help rid the world of abominations like this guy.

He's got a point about not hurting the living, though.

It's sick. It's cannibalism.

Since he was a ghoul, it would technically only be cannibalism if he ate other ghouls.

Before he managed to sort it out, Gordon perched on the edge of one of the big chairs. Richard could hardly leave him sitting there alone. Reluctantly, he holstered his gun and lowered himself into the seat next to his partner. The springs gave way under his butt, and he sank just about all the way to the floor. Good Lord, there'd be no graceful way of getting out of this thing. He cleared his throat and tried to gather some semblance of dignity around himself.

"Tell us what you know," Richard said to regain the upper hand.

The doctor eyed him for a moment before answering. "I know that you're hunters in a land of monsters, and your CDC guise is pathetic. What do you know?"

"How did you know we were hunters?" Gordon asked.

Dr. Lewis smiled, showing off his perfectly human-looking fake teeth. "I've been around longer than you might imagine. One does not reach this age by being naive." He picked up a cheap Bic pen and twirled it between his fingers. "There was another case similar to this one a generation or so ago. Hunters came then, as well. History repeats."

"That case didn't end well," Gordon said.

"No?" The pen tapped against the desk calendar. "The deaths came to an end, did they not?"

"Apparently not."

"Touché." He laid the pen down, carefully lining it up

parallel with the edge of the paper. "I don't know what is killing the children, but it's not the same as before."

Richard tried to lean forward. A spring gave way and poked him in the butt. He shifted with a grumble. "Looks the same to us."

"You don't have all the information." He reached for a stack of file folders in a black metal tray and slid them across the desk.

Gordon took the folders and read.

Thoughts and questions blew through Richard's brain like dandelion fluff on a windy spring day. He latched onto one of them. "If the monsters up here are all trying to lay low, this kind of killing—the kind that catches the attention of hunters— would have you nervous as a pregnant possum."

"You might find this hard to believe, but we monsters have a code of ethics by which we live."

"Hard to believe" was an understatement. Monsters fed on humanity. Some of them had gone so far as to try to set up a human farm on Mars. Where was the code of ethics in that? He harrumphed in response.

"The first batch faded in bursts. These kids go downhill fast from day one. There're never more than a few weeks between the first complaints and the deaths," Gordon said. He was flipping from one folder to another, his eyes darting left and right. His words rang a bell. Stan had said something similar.

"You're quick with details," the doctor said to Gordon. He faced Richard. "But I suspect you already know the answer. You just haven't quite wrapped your mind around it yet."

The fluff of thoughts piled up and drifted like snow. Richard scowled, trying to make sense of it then as if a light- ning strike had blown away everything but the truth, he had it in his grasp. "Something is doing this on purpose and trying to make it look like Stanley's old case. They wanted him to come here."

"I don't know who Stanley is, but I think you've hit the proverbial nail on the head."

Gordon slammed the files shut. "It's a trap."

The ghoul gave a slow nod. "I don't know about all that, but I'd suspect something along those lines, yes."

No punch in the gut could have knocked the wind out of Richard so effectively. *A trap.*

"We've got to find them." God only knew why Stanley and Burke had wandered into the forest, but Richard would be a damned fool not to follow them. Twenty-four hours indeed.

Friggin' Stan Kapcheck.

Flailing like an overturned beetle didn't help get Richard out of the low-slung chair, so when Gordon offered a hand, he latched on with good grace and let the younger man pull him to his feet.

"Gentlemen," the doctor leaned back in his chair.

They both stopped to look at him. "I suggest you tread lightly. Ridding us of our problematic community member is a favor, but tensions run high when hunters are in the area."

"That some kind of a threat?" Richard asked.

"Just making sure you fully understand the situation. We want this mystery solved, too, but we would like it to be accomplished with a modicum of discretion."

Getting to Port Angeles from the cabin had taken an hour and fifteen minutes. Gordon managed the return trip in under an hour. Gordon's eyes remained fixed on the road. They didn't speak.

Richard stared out the window and tried to sort his thoughts. *Something is doing this on purpose and trying to make it look like Stanley's old case. They wanted him to come here.*

Had he really known that all along? If so, why had he gone along with the plan? Why had he left Burke with Stanley? Why hadn't he gone after them last night?

"I didn't know." He hadn't intended to say it out loud, but

there it was. Might as well finish the thought. "It wasn't until you said that about the kids that everything started to make sense. I was just going along with Stanley's plan."

"Stanley always has a plan," Gordon mumbled.

Richard pushed his false teeth around inside his mouth and pondered that. Back when they met, Stanley had a plan to meet Richard. When monsters attacked, Stanley had a plan to get them out of the old folks' home. Stanley had a plan to fight El Chupacabra along the banks of some river in the South Dakota mountains. That one hadn't turned out so well, so they'd ended up in the hospital with their car missing. As soon as they had a second to catch their breath, Stanley started making a new plan that pulled Burke into their little posse. On and on it went.

Stanley always had a plan.

Wherever he went with Burke, he wasn't wandering around blindly following his nose. He had a plan before he ever agreed to come to this place. The plan involved sending Richard and Gordon into town so he could go out into the woods and do whatever he meant to do there, and he wanted a full twenty-four hours to get it done.

Why had he sent them away?

A discontented grumble rolled through Richard's gut, and he realized they'd failed to pick up any lunch while they were in town. He'd have to make do with sandwich fixings at the cabin. No way was he going back to the over-priced frou-frou joint they'd been at the night before.

Shoving thoughts of his empty stomach aside, he shared the conclusion he'd drawn with Gordon. "Stan knew it was a trap. He sent us away so that if he fell into it, we'd be free to save his skinny butt."

Gordon threw a quick, skeptical glance in Richard's direction. "He planned to get caught by the monsters?"

"It ain't the first time," Richard said.

"So, if we go where he told us, won't we be falling into the same trap?"

"Not if he told us to go somewhere different from where he really went."

Gordon loosed a string of creative curses. Richard didn't judge him. He knew all too well that hanging around Stan Kapcheck could have that effect on a person.

CHAPTER SIXTEEN

Burke

A year ago, Burke spent every night alone in a king-sized bed. She slept on top of the best memory foam mattress money could buy, wrapped in a cocoon of high-thread-count sheets beneath a down comforter. To her, the luxury of a comfortable nest to sleep in seemed to be part of normal life. She took it for granted.

Since the day her grandfather called her to help him and Stanley, she'd slept in cheap motel beds with scratchy blankets that smelled of things she'd rather not think about. She'd slept in the Cadillac more times than she could count. She'd slept on the floor of a magically warded cage, but until she lay half-frozen on the forest floor, pain throbbing in her injured arm, did she give genuine thought to the fantastic bed she'd given up. Would she ever own a bed like that again? Would she buy a house and settle down with Gordon and walk her dog and tend her garden?

Would I even survive to see Gordon again?

That question and others just as unanswerable plagued her

as she drifted in and out of restless sleep. At the first hint of the new day edging in the dark corners of the night, she sat up and stretched. She considered building a fire, but for what purpose? They had no food to cook.

Stanley stirred beside her, stretched like a cat, and sat up. He brushed the pine needles from his clothes. "How's your shoulder, my dear?"

Her shoulder throbbed in unison with the beat of her heart. "If someone offered me heroin right now, I'd consider it a viable option."

He nodded and rubbed a hand over his mouth. "I'm sorry, Burke. For—"

"Don't." She stopped him before he could go into the list of things he was sorry for. "I'm a grown-up. There's nothing happening here that I didn't sign up for." *More or less.*

She used her good hand to push off the ground and bit her bottom lip to stifle any undignified noises. Then she managed to get to her feet. "What's next?"

Stanley remained seated with his feet planted in front of him and his elbows propped on his knees. His gaze roamed over the hills and trees. "Busar isn't killing those children."

"Yeah. I gathered that." Gingerly, Burke stretched again. Moving worked the kinks out and warmed the blood that felt like slush in her veins, but moving the wrong way would be disastrous when she was managing her pain with nothing more than willpower.

"He could help us." Stanley's eyes finally stilled. He studied her reaction.

What could she say to Stanley when she could barely comprehend what was wrong with him? Taking a page from his playbook, she answered his statement with a question. "Is having his help worth the risk?"

More gracefully than she had done, he got to his feet. "No, it's not, not when I consider the bones of the creatures who died for no reason other than his presence. It's as if his curse has ripened with time."

"It's not a curse, though."

Stanley checked his weapons and patted his pockets. "Explain, please."

It wasn't the first time she had to find a way to think past pain, but she didn't remember it ever being quite so challenging. "I mean, it's not literally a curse. It's an imbalance, so it makes sense that it's getting worse. It's like a tear in fabric. Once it starts, more and more of the threads at the edge are going to unravel. It's inevitable that it will grow worse. It's been decades."

Stanley nodded. "I believe you're right. But that argues for not leaving him here."

"I don't follow."

"What will his condition be in another thirty years? In a hundred? Five hundred? I believe he told us the truth. He's jailed himself so completely that the earth will fall down around him before he is set free, but he is immortal, immutable. The earth is not. It will fall down around him, and some future generation will suffer dire consequences."

"But if we let him out now, this generation will suffer dire consequences."

No self-pity or shame shone in Stanley's eyes when he made his confession. "I don't know what to do. I have never known what to do about this, so I've done nothing. But that, too, is a choice with terrible consequences."

Something scratched Burke's neck. She reached up and pulled a small twig from the collar of her jacket. "How about if we agree that we will do something, take some action to solve the problem of Busar, but we deal with our problems one at a time. Hunters are led to their hunt, right? At this moment, Busar is no threat to anything other than wildlife that wanders too close, but we know that something is killing children. Let's find our killer and save those kids."

"And then I will stay until the problem of Busar is solved."

"You mean we'll all stay," Burke corrected.

Stanley's eyes twinkled. "You give me hope on the grayest of days."

Based on the pathetic light reaching them, the day could literally be the grayest of days.

He released a breath. "Let's talk to Busar. We'll assure him that we're not leaving him."

Busar did not come to the bars of his cage, and Stanley did not descend to the valley's floor a second time.

"I won't leave you again," Stanley called out.

"Then you will die in this place," Busar replied from the darkness.

If Burke didn't know better, she'd say Stanley sounded almost relieved when he answered. "So be it."

CHAPTER SEVENTEEN

Richard

STANLEY TOLD THEM THE FOREST WAS HOME TO JUST ABOUT every kind of ghost and goblin, so what should they take with them? Richard wished they could drive the Caddy in. There was a lot to be said for having an entire armory on wheels.

"Wish in one hand, poop in the other," he mumbled.

Gordon looked up from the bag he was packing on the kitchen counter. "What's that?"

"Ain't talking to you," Richard said.

He loaded silver bullets in his gun. Silver took care of many things, including the things that could be killed by plain old brass casings. An iron blade didn't hold an edge worth a snot, but it would slice through ghosts and fairies like butter. He clipped the knife to his belt. There'd be no shortage of sticks in the woods, but there was no guarantee those at hand in a crisis would be sharp enough or strong enough to get the job done if it came to that, so he put four wooden stakes in the messenger bag hanging from his shoulder. He added a folding hunting knife and a lighter. Neither would do a thing against monsters, but if they got lost and spent the night in the forest, they'd be happy to have both.

"Going slow, it still shouldn't take more than an hour and a half at most to get there," Gordon said.

Who asked him? Richard scowled. He wasn't all that slow. He was a good measure faster than he had been a year ago. Give the ex-marine another forty years on this earth, knock him off a curb, and have a doctor stick his hip full of pins, and then see how fast he was. Still, while Richard was plenty spry, it might be a good idea to find a walking stick along the way. He wouldn't be any help to anyone if his droopy leg dragged on the ground, got his toe caught under a tree root, and sent him sprawling.

He glanced out the window. The sun hung low over the ocean. "We best get a move on, then."

Half an hour later, standing next to the Cadillac on the side of the road, shotgun slung over his shoulder and a compass in his hand, Gordon pointed toward the dense growth across the street. "Two miles, straight ahead."

No matter that he found a perfect walking stick twenty yards in, Richard was forced to admit that the going was slow. Picking their way through patches of ferns that grew tall and dense as any Midwest cornfield and weaving to the left and right of trees big enough to drive a car through, every yard of eastward progress was bought at a steep price of time and energy.

Their shadows, cast from behind by the faint light of the sun filtered through clouds and canopy, stretched long and sinuous as serpents in front of them.

Life around them rustled and buzzed. A few of the creatures scampered around them. Richard had no doubt the creatures saw them. Maybe it would be a good idea to get his gun out and carry it in his free hand. Then again, maybe not. If he did trip and take a fall, it would be just his luck to shoot himself on the way down.

Sharp upward slopes and long downward inclines did not make the walk any easier. All said and done, more than two hours passed before Gordon gestured with the compass and said, "Over there, another fifty yards or so."

They followed a relatively clear stretch of dirt that wound around the lower edge of a small hill toward the coordinates Stanley had left them.

"Cripes, almighty," Richard declared when he saw what awaited them.

Gordon's arm fell to his side. "What is it?"

A perfect circle was blasted into the earth, as if by an asteroid or an alien spaceship with jets a hundred feet across. Within the circle, only the composted remains of long-dead vegetation remained. Despite the beads of sweat the exercise drawn on his brow, Richard's guts turned to ice.

"It's unhallowed ground." The broken, wasted tree trunks caught Richard's eye. "But—"

"What does that mean?"

Richard rolled his eyes. Why did he get stuck training the new guy? It wasn't his boyfriend. Careful not to step into the ruined area, Richard picked his way around the edge of the circle, looking for anything that might offer an answer instead of just more questions. "Look here." With his walking stick, he tapped a ledge of earth, like a tiny six-inch dam, built around the outside of the circle. "And those tree trunks there, they form some kind of crooked triangle."

"I see it," Gordon said.

"Not many things can cause a patch of unhallowed ground like this. I mean, a single grave, an altar site, sure, but something this big," Richard fiddled with his hearing aid so it would stop giving him feedback every time a bird screeched. "I only ever saw anything like this once, back in Louisiana. Only half this size, though. And I've seen pictures in the lore."

"Is this different?"

Richard nodded. "Every other time I've seen it, everything is pushed away. Looks almost like everything alive, even the plants, jumped away from whatever happened."

"This looks more like it was crushed by some immense force."

"What the Sam Hill did Stan want to come out here for?" Richard wondered.

Before either of them could come up with even a half-cocked answer to that question, an ephemeral form shimmered into sight on the other side of the circle.

"Ghost," Richard called. He snatched the iron blade from its holster, glad now that he'd thought to bring it, even if it was heavy as a tub of lard.

Gordon pulled the shotgun into his arms and chambered a round.

The ghosts snarled and came closer—close enough that its form grew clear to see. Wisps of fur surrounded a snarling face. Ghostly teeth snapped at them.

Richard's heart seized in his chest so painfully it knocked the wind out of him. As a result, he sounded like a wheezy asthmatic when he said, "Son of a biscuit, it ain't a human ghost. It's a blasted werewolf."

Gordon pulled the trigger, and the gun roared, sending a spray of salt pellets into the creature. Snarling, it burst into smoke and dissipated.

"I ain't never—

But Richard didn't get a chance to tell Gordon what he had never seen before Gordon fired again, this time into a shimmering white vampire. Even before the remains drifted away, two more creatures resembling angry trees with teeth appeared, shimmering, white, and translucent.

Gordon lowered the gun to reload, and one of the things came at them. Richard stepped forward and swiped with the knife. It burst apart, sending a wash of icy-cold air over them.

Six creatures now.

Two shots and a swipe of the knife, a frigid wind from the one that exploded at arm's length. Teeth and claws every which way.

Now there were ten.

"Richard?"

"What?"

"We've got to do something," Burke's genius boyfriend suggested.

"You can slap my butt and call me Sally if you got any ideas."

"We run, maybe?"

Run? Wouldn't it make more sense to stay and figure out what they came for?

Twelve ghost monsters, twenty-four glittering eyes, and more teeth than Richard could count, all focused on them. A freezing cold hand, tipped with razor claws, dug into the upper part of Richard's left arm. Pain ripped through him. He jabbed with the iron knife. The pressure disappeared, but the bloody cuts remained.

Gordon fired twice in quick succession.

No way to count how many of these things were coming at them now.

A sudden change of heart came over Richard. "Run!"

They turned to run and smashed into an invisible barrier that knocked them flat on their butts. At some point, without intending to do so, they'd stepped into the circle, and now that they were in it, they couldn't get out.

A spirit looking like the bowrow he'd killed in the early days with Stanley thumped into his chest like a glacier crashing against the Titanic, knocking the wind out of him. He slashed sideways, and the iron made quick work of his attacker, but when he sat up, an army of spirit monsters stood waiting to take the defeated creature's place.

CHAPTER EIGHTEEN

Burke

THROUGH YEARS OF YOGA AND MARTIAL ARTS TRAINING, Burke learned that pain is not real. It has no substance. By itself, pain can't kill you or inflict any lasting damage. It is simply a message from your nervous system that something is wrong.

In her case, she knew too well what was wrong. A vampire with enough hair to pass for a werewolf had flipped her upside down and dropped her on her shoulder, breaking her collarbone clean in two. Stanley had reset the break, and she had faith that he'd done it well. One learns such skills in a hundred years of hunting, but that didn't keep her body from sending her ever more urgent messages about her injury.

She drew in each breath through her nose to a slow count of five and released through a slim opening in her lips to the same count.

Again and again, heading due north, she placed one foot in front of the other and ignored the messages.

"There." Stanley pointed at nothing ahead. "We've nearly made it, just like I said."

It took several more steps before Burke understood what he was talking about, but then she saw it, too—a change in the quality of light, a thinning of the canopy up ahead.

With her next breath, she caught the scent of salt. They'd drawn near to the coast again.

Stanley postulated that, from just about any point in the forest, if a person walked north, they'd come to the body of water that separates the state of Washington from Canada's Vancouver Island. Highway 101 runs along the length of that coastline. No matter if they were near civilization or not, a car was bound to come along the highway at some point. They could beg for help in getting back to the cabin or at least use a phone to call Richard and Gordon to get them.

As they drew closer to the road, Stanley chuckled.

"You're amused?" Burke was not amused, but she'd gladly take the distraction of a good joke.

"I know where we are," Stanley said.

The news annoyed her further rather than bring her a smile. "I'm glad somebody knows where we are."

"See that?" He gestured toward a brick wall, barely visible between the tree trunks.

Burke confirmed that she saw it.

"That is a Jehovah's Witness's Kingdom Hall. I've been there."

"Were you saved?"

Stanley glanced at her with a twinkle in his eye. "In a manner of speaking."

Burke didn't know what that meant and wasn't about to ask. If it had something to do with a lover, she might get sick.

One foot in front of the other, the forest gave way to a weedy lawn, cut down to within an inch of the hard brown soil.

The lawn led to a blacktop parking lot in the center of which sprouted a brown brick building with a brown roof surrounded by brown landscaping stones. Even though she couldn't see it, in Burke's imagination, a brown sign beside the road declared that this was the Kingdom Hall.

A woman in a long denim skirt with metal buttons running the length of it and a puffy pink sweater that hung past her hips picked bits of trash from the rocks and stuffed them in a plastic bag. As they approached, she stood and turned in their direction. Her warm smile seemed to say that she greeted filthy, bedraggled strangers staggering out of the woods every day.

"Hello." She folded her hands together, and the green and white Dollar Tree bag swung gently in the breeze coming off the water.

"Good afternoon," Stanley said. "I happened upon this lovely church several years ago and made the acquaintance of Stonewall Phillips. He was the elder here at that time, as I understood it."

The girl tugged the sleeves of her sweater down over her hands. She could have been seventeen or thirty with her plain, pretty, unlined face. "That's my father. He's inside. Would you like to talk with him?"

Stanley clapped his hands together like a man who just made the world's most clever guess and won a prize at the state fair. "I would like that very much, thank you."

Inside the church, warm, dry air wrapped around Burke like a mother's arms, and she fought the urge to curl up in the nearest corner and go to sleep. Instead of giving in, focused on the spot between Stanley's shoulder blades and let his movement draw her past rows of cream-colored stackable chairs with shiny metal legs.

"As I live and breathe, it can't possibly be." The gentle tenor voice carried a hint of a southern drawl. "Stanley Kapcheck?"

Stanley chuckled and walked faster. "Words cannot convey how pleased I am to stumble into your little church here."

The preacher took in Stanley's appearance—slightly wrinkled with a dab of dust on one cheek—and then looked at Burke. She hadn't seen herself, but judging from his words, she hadn't fared the restless night as well as Stan did.

"Well, you look like you've gone ten rounds with a bear in the forest."

"You're not so far off," Stanley admitted. He stepped to the side and introduced Burke to a balding man with a slender frame and eyes the color of coffee with cream. "This is my associate, Burke Martin."

"Pleased to meet you, Mr. Phillips." Thank God her parents had drilled manners so deep into her during her childhood. No way she'd be able to fake some politeness right now if it weren't a rote habit.

Stonewall Phillips looked back and forth between the two beggars who stood before him. His brows arched down over his gentle eyes. "Tell me you haven't been lost out there in the forest."

"Not lost, exactly. It's more like we found ourselves a little farther in than we intended. When we popped out, I was delighted to see that it was right here in your lovely little territory."

The man clucked with concern like a mother hen. "And you're hurt, to boot." He gestured at Burke's arm. "Sit, please sit." Turning his attention to his daughter, he asked her to find hot drinks and something to eat.

Burke flopped into one of the padded chairs and wondered if anyone would judge her for toppling over and going to sleep. As she contemplated the idea, the elder of the Kingdom Hall said just about the only thing that could flood her with enough adrenaline to wake her again.

"I owe you my life, Stanley, but if you're here because of my girl, I'll fight you to the death. She's a natural-born and no business of yours."

Natural-born?

Stanley's draped a casual arm around Burke's shoulders and squeezed gently. "I had no idea you and Phyllis had a child. My congratulations. She's lovely."

"And gentle as the day is long." The other man's shoulders relaxed, and he turned a chair to sit and face them.

"I have no doubt, raised by people such as her parents are," Stanley assured him.

"You really did just wander into this place by accident? You're honest with me?"

In a handful of incidences, Burke had met "monsters" who were doing no harm but living their lives the best way they knew how. None of them had been shifters, but she had to admit she hadn't met enough of them to say whether they were a violent race. After all, they chased the violent ones. The others could live their lives undetected if they chose to do so. "Perhaps we were led to you," she said.

He nodded. "Jehovah does work in such a way, in my experience. A long time ago, Stanley solved a difficult problem for me and my kind. He saved lives at great personal cost. Perhaps I'm now given a chance to repay his selflessness. Tell me what you need."

Just then, the shifter girl returned carrying a plastic tray laden with mugs of tea and saltine crackers. In all Burke's life, no refreshment had ever looked better. Her words of thanks came automatically. Resisting the urge to cram the crackers in her mouth and chug the steaming liquid required more effort. The tea ran down her parched throat and unfurled its warmth in her belly as if it were the nectar of the gods.

Even Stanley drank much deeper than his usual proper sips

before speaking again. "Really, all we need is a ride, but it's kind of a long way. South of Forks."

"I'd be happy to take you, but I must admit, I doubt that's all you need," Stonewall said.

Stanley grinned over the brim of his mug. "It's all I'll ask, for now, but I wouldn't say no to a second cup of tea and your phone number." He shrugged. "Just in case."

CHAPTER NINETEEN

Richard

RICHARD HELD HIS KNIFE OUT IN FRONT OF HIM, KNOWING full well it would be as effective against this angry mob of monsters as pissing on a forest fire. He stepped back, eager to put distance between them and himself, and stumbled over the raised edge of the blackened circle.

As it does in moments of disaster, time stopped allowing him to analyze his thoughts. He remembered tripping over the door jamb on his way into the cabin.

Stumbling.

Doors.

Steps.

"It's a door!"

Gordon fired two shots in quick succession. "What?"

"It's not unhallowed ground; it's a doorway, man."

A ghostly hand seized Richard's throat. He jabbed his knife into the air where a belly would be, and the form burst apart, leaving him half-frozen and choking.

"How do we shut it?" Gordon demanded.

How the heck was he supposed to know? He did have one trick, though. "I can't shut it, but I can...here. Take this." He thrust the handle of his knife into Gordon's hand. Now wasn't the time for long-winded explanations. "Cover me."

He stepped out of the circle, shrugged off the pack, and laid hands on a large can of salt. The thing had been a bugger to carry. Weighed as much as a dead priest, but if it worked, it was worth it.

"Step back."

Gordon slashed at the two ghosts charging them before hopping out of the circle. Moving as fast as his tin can hip joint would allow, Richard stepped in front of him, drawing a line of salt along the edge of the "doorway".

"Trade me." Gordon snatched the can from Richard's hands and gave him the knife, leaving the now-empty shotgun on the ground. The younger man raced along the outside of the circle, enclosing their attackers.

Well, most of their attackers. Four of them managed to squeak out of the circle ahead of him. Richard slashed left and right like a maniac, making quick work of the ghosts, and sending stabbing pains along his upper back. Four more tried to follow but slammed up against the salt line as if it were a dome made of shatterproof glass.

Richard's heart hammered in his chest.

"It worked." Gordon sounded surprised.

"'Course it worked." Richard was a little surprised, too, but he wasn't about to admit that he'd risked both their butts on a wild guess.

"You don't think Stanley and Burke are...?" Gordon gestured vaguely toward the riling, snarling mass of white ephemeral forms.

Richard scowled. "Nah. Stan would have known what this was when he saw it."

"So, why did he send us here?"

"Blast if I know." He ran his fingers through his hair, pressing it down against his scalp where it would stay for at least three-and-a-half seconds.

What would Stanley do if they were in a place and a bunch of monsters tried to get in and kill them? Such a thing had happened nearly half a dozen times by Richard's count.

"Stanley would lock the door," he said.

"Okay. How?"

"Not with a key, that's for dang sure." Could he remember the locking spell without screwing it up?

He looked around. "I need a pile of kindling. Big enough to make a little fire and some bones. Whatever you can find. Owl pellet or something. We got salt and the rest.

Gordon trotted off to do his bidding, and Richard didn't feel any twinge of guilt in letting the other man do the physical work. His old body had had just about enough excitement for one day, and it wasn't over yet. Magic had a way of taking it out of you, and they still had to haul their butts back to the cabin, assuming they managed to stay alive long enough to do that.

While Gordon rummaged around the forest floor looking for the remains of some poor, unfortunate creature, Richard lowered himself to the earth with all the care of a dynamite expert lowering a stick of sweating TNT into a pre-drilled hole. His joints popped in protest, but he managed to get onto his butt and sit splay-legged like a toddler playing on the floor.

Ignoring the growling, screaming mass that now looked more like riling smoke in a glass jar than individual creatures with distinct forms, he cleared away the debris on the ground directly in front of him, even using the iron blade to root up a few tenacious little weeds. He smoothed the damp soil, pressing down gently until it was dark and uniform as a chalkboard. Then, using the blade again, he drew the best circle he could manage and marked the edges with basic runes. Burke could draw the fancy ones, but simple was good enough to get the job done in this case. He hoped.

Making sure not to break the line, Richard stole a few pinches of salt from what Gordon had poured and sprinkled them in the center of the circle before building a teepee of sticks over it.

Gritting his false teeth together so hard the plastic plates bit into his gums, he dragged the blade of his real knife across the outside of his forearm until a little line of blood appeared. Half a dozen drops splattered onto the kindling before the cut dried up. Heck, if he knew why the idiots in Hollywood always showed a guy cutting into the meat of his palm to get a few drops of blood. A person stupid enough to injure their own hand on purpose would be dead before their first hunt started.

He peeked up at the boiling pot of monster ghost stew. Did he even know that monsters had spirits that could get trapped like ghosts before this moment? As far as he remembered, nothing like that had come up in the lore, and Stanley never mentioned it—though a mention might have been nice before sending them out here.

Of course, there was the distinct possibility Stan sent them to this spot without really knowing what was here. That would be a very Stanley sort of thing to do. After all, this is the same man that got his leg busted up when he told Richard they were headed out to hunt El Chupacabra and ended up fighting a man-eating serpent with stubby little arms instead. Now, knowing what he knew, Richard puzzled over how an experienced hunter like Stanley could have made that mistake. It should have been crystal clear from the—

"Will this work?" Gordon came busting out of the woods like a bull, carrying the remains of some poor, unfortunate bird in his palms.

Richard nodded and pointed at the crude bowl formed by the sticks at the top of the teepee of kindling. Gordon laid the bones there so gently it was like he was trying not to wake the creature back to life.

With a deep breath, Richard sent up a prayer to the Almighty to help him get the Latin right and lit the fire. Then he began chanting. The dirt under his butt shifted like the whole planet had shivered, and an unearthly wail rose from the dead—or the undead—or the dead again—or whatever they were.

Flames snapped and popped within the twigs before growing unnaturally bright. They licked at the bones like greedy little tongues of heat. Richard said the words again and again, careful to say them just the way Stanley did in his memory.

Again, the world trembled. White light shot out of the doorway of dead space and slammed back into the ground with the force of a comet falling from some distant reach of the galaxy.

If he hadn't been sitting down, Richard would have been blown clear off his feet. He covered his face with his arms as debris rained down around him. When the ruckus ended, he peeked around his elbow and saw Gordon lying in the dirt next to him.

"All right?" Richard asked.

Gordon blinked like a startled owlet and sat up. He scowled. "A warning would have been nice."

Richard shrugged. "I didn't know that was going to happen. Ain't never seen a thing like that in my life."

"Did it work?"

They both peered straight ahead. There was nothing much to be seen, just a wide crater, and on the other side of it, trees, and more trees.

"Looks like," Richard said.

Getting to his feet required more than half a minute and the full measure of his attention, but he managed, and for that, he gave himself a mental pat on the back. Not a lot of guys over eighty could do the things he did. There was Stanley, but he was a freak of nature, so he didn't count.

He edged up to the salt line and looked in both directions like a kid fixing to cross a street after his mama told him not to.

Trees to the left.

Trees to the right.

No ghosts or monsters in sight—not that it meant they weren't there.

With one foot, he stepped across the salt line, tapped the edge of the hole with his toe, and drew back.

Nothing happened.

Gordon tapped his arm. "Look. What is that?"

Following his pointed finger, Richard squinted at the single object in the exact center of the blast zone. Maybe eight inches tall, thin, white, it appeared to be ivory or bone.

"Stay here. I'll go." Gordon stepped over the salt and paused.

Richard waited, so nervous he was sweating like a whore in church under his warm winter coat.

Nothing happened.

Gordon turned his body sideways and slip-skip-ran down the steep hill of loose dirt churned up from whatever power blew away the relatively smooth surface that had been there before. He crouched over the object and reached for it.

"Don't touch it," Richard shouted.

Drawing back his hand as if from a fire, Gordon almost lost his balance but made a decent recovery.

"What's it look like?" Richard asked.

"Bone, I think. It's carved all over. I swear the drawings look like aliens. I've never seen anything like it."

"For the love of God, man, do not touch it."

"What is it?"

"Heck if I know. Hold on." It took a minute of rummaging,

but Richard came up with a scrap of leather stuffed in the bottom of the pack. "Use this to pick it up."

Once the mysterious object had been safely retrieved, Gordon scrambled back out of the crater and over the salt line, careful to keep the line intact. He held out his finding, and Richard studied it. True enough, the carvings along the length of the thing did look like aliens. It was hard to see, though. While they'd dealt with whatever gateway to hell Stanley sent them into, the sun slipped below the horizon, and the light was all but gone.

"I'll look at it later." He flipped the edges of the cloth over the relic. "That spell won't keep anything shut forever, and we'd do well to get out of here before we end up spending the night in the forest."

Without arguing, Gordon slipped the little package into the backpack along with the other items that had spilled out. He lifted it up, and Richard shrugged into it, choking down his complaints about carrying the thing. If he was strong enough to get it out here, he was strong enough to get it back to the cabin again.

Flicking his phone's flashlight on, he turned to find himself looking straight into red, glowing eyes. He fumbled for his gun, and a growl rolled through the night, but not from the seven-foot-tall creature directly in front of him—from their right, where an identical beast peeked out from behind a tree.

"Two to your left," Gordon said.

Jesus H. Cripes, Almighty, how many battles could a man expect to fight in a single day?

He drew his weapon at last and prepared to do what he must. After all, what else could a man do? At least if he lost, he'd go down in a blaze of glory.

CHAPTER TWENTY

Burke

STANLEY THANKED STONEWALL FOR THE RIDE, THEN SAID, "Maybe you could hang around just long enough for us to make sure everything's okay inside?"

The preacher grinned. "Want me to hold your hand and tuck you in like a little girl?"

"Well, if you're offering," Stanley replied with a twinkle in his eye.

Stonewall shook his head and chuckled while Stanley climbed out of the old Jeep Cherokee and extended a hand to help Burke.

Burke let Stan go ahead, knowing her reflexes were shot from exhaustion and pain.

He stood at the bottom of the stairs, studying every part of the porch, then leaned to the right to inspect something that caught his eye. Everything must have passed inspection because he trotted up the steps and pushed the door open before pausing again and disappearing inside.

After a moment, he returned and waved toward the truck. "All clear. Thanks again."

"It's nothing. My debt is still owed." With a tip of his head, Stonewall said goodbye and reversed out of the driveway onto the highway.

Stanley squatted and pointed to the spot to the immediate right of the steps. "What do you make of that?"

Burke stood on the first stair and could see the perfect circle burned into the weather-beaten boards. "Remains of a hex bag?"

Stanley nodded.

"It could have been there since before we came. It's a pretty tucked-away spot. Maybe none of us noticed it."

"Do you believe that?" he asked.

She confessed that she did not. "Do you think someone magicked us to Busar?"

He stood and slipped his hands into his jacket pockets. "All evidence points to that."

"Why?"

"I'm sure I don't know. We shall add that to our list of mysteries to be solved. At the moment, I'm more concerned about finding your grandfather and Gordon."

Burke's exhausted heart withered up like a moldy raisin. "They're not here?"

"I'm afraid not. I believe they've gone looking for us in the place I intended for us to go."

Looking over her shoulder, she confirmed what she'd already seen. "But the car is here."

"It's not a place you can drive. It's in the forest."

A host of responses flitted across the back of Burke's tongue.

You go. I'll wait here.

We lived through the night out there. They will, too.

What the hell is wrong with you, sending an old man and a noob into a forest full of monsters?

At last, she actually spoke. "Explain, please."

"Let's go inside and get some proper food. I'll explain while we eat."

Over sandwiches and fresh coffee, Stanley made good on his promise. "When we were talking before, you mentioned that even a tiny, relatively harmless bite could leave a scar for life. It occurred to me that, while the magic we had turned out to be too unstable to properly meet our needs at the time, it was, nonetheless, fantastically powerful."

Burke nodded understanding, her mouth too full to allow her to speak. Had turkey and tomatoes ever, in the entire history of the world, ever tasted so good? The mayonnaise was the creamiest she'd ever eaten. The lettuce broke, crisp and fresh, over her tongue. It was the most delicious sandwich since the Earl of Sandwich slapped some beef between two slices of bread and called it a good thing. The fact that the extra-strength Tylenol kicked in only added to her overwhelming contentment. If she'd taken the more potent stuff, she probably would have passed out from the satisfaction of it all.

"Look at what some little hex bag did to the floorboards outside," Stanley said. "Magic, such as we used, would make an impression on the earth that might never fade away. I thought, perhaps if we could go to the place where the spell was performed, we could find some sort of clue as to what energy or entity survived, or perhaps," he shrugged and sipped his coffee. "Something, I don't know, but anything that might point us in the right direction. Would you like another sandwich, dear? I'll be happy to make it for you."

She looked down at her empty plate. *Dang. How had that happened?* Since Stanley had already gotten to his feet and pulled two slices of bread from the plastic bag, she let him carry on with it.

He talked while he worked. "You pointed out that it would be prudent to let our associates know where we were headed, so I sent them the coordinates. After a moment's thought, I asked them to give us twenty-four hours."

"That's a long time to search a small area." The strong coffee washed down her throat and steamed in her belly, sending fabulous little zaps of energy into her bloodstream. She considered the possibility that coffee possessed magical properties. What else could bring her back to life so quickly?

"Agreed." Stanley set the plate in front of her. "But, again, I had no idea what we were looking for—if anything. I thought we'd be back that same evening. If we weren't, I didn't want them stumbling around in the forest trying to find us in the dark."

She glanced toward the west-facing window where the flaming circle of the sun was neatly framed. "Which they're going to be doing, very soon, anyway."

"And when they get to the coordinates, there will be no sign of us, so what will they do? Return here to wait, or start searching in that vast wilderness to figure out what happened to us? The place where we were was miles from there. It would take days to make the hike, assuming they knew to go straight to that location."

"How could they know that?" The second sandwich didn't quite live up to the first, but she had no complaints.

"They couldn't."

"Whatever the thing is that you thought we might find there, the scar or whatever, if they see it, will they recognize it as important?"

Stanley cocked his head. "I have a great deal of faith in your grandfather."

"He's come a long way," Burke agreed.

"He's a natural. Not many take to this life as easily as the two of you have."

She felt compelled to state the obvious. "But he's an old man with all the baggage old age demands. We can't just leave him out there. Gordon knows how to survive in normal human circumstances, but this is more than that."

"Indeed." Stanley rose, then cleared, rinsed, and stacked the dishes neatly in the sink. "You're ready to go, then?"

The words had the effect of poking a tiny hole in a balloon. She sagged in her chair and lied. "So ready. I've been waiting for the chance. Let's roll." She pushed her chair back and willed herself to her feet. "I don't care if you do say it's a short hike. This time, we're taking provisions."

Stanley propped a hip against the counter and dried his hand on a white towel adorned with yellow daisies. "Agreed, and upon further reflection, we left under-armed last time. We'll take the big guns." He hung the towel from the oven's handle and adjusted the edges so they lined up. "Just in case."

CHAPTER TWENTY-ONE

Richard

RICHARD TOOK SOME ASSURANCE FROM HAVING GORDON'S back pressed against his. At least nothing would get him from behind without him being warned.

"Why aren't they coming any closer?" Gordon asked.

"Heck if I know."

The same question pricked Richard's consciousness. No matter that he and Gordon were armed. Their weapons would be no match for this bunch of teeth and fur. By his count, ten of the things snarled at them from every direction. Each towered taller than any human, had more teeth than any shark, and sported claws like eagle's talons. Maybe the guns would slow them down, but they'd never take the whole pack in a fair fight. The only way he could think of to get out would be to cast a spell that blew them backward, but he'd have to find a good number of ingredients before he could perform that kind of magic and....

Truth smacked into his mind like a bag full of bricks. *Magic.*

"It's the totem."

"I don't follow." Gordon shifted slightly to the left.

Richard shuffled his feet to keep their backs together. "That thing you found is the totem Stan's been going on about. Thing is powerful as the staff of Moses. They're scared of it. That's why they're not coming closer."

Gordon seemed to chew on that information for a few moments.

The nearest monster, the only one Richard could see in the glow of the phone's light, edged closer, scared but not entirely put off, still testing to see if there was a way to reach their quarry.

"Do you know how to use it?" Gordon asked.

Richard threw a glance over his shoulder. "You're a few pickles short of a barrel if you think I'm going to use that thing. Last guy who messed with that thing got his soul ripped in half, in case you ain't heard that story yet."

"Okay, then, they're scared to approach it. If we just start walking, maybe they'll keep their distance."

"If a frog had wings, maybe he wouldn't bump his butt on the ground." Richard blinked hard and squinted, trying to see into the shadows. "Besides, we still don't have a clue where Burke and Stanley are. We go back to the cabin; what good can we do them there?"

"What good will it do them for us to spend the night in the woods, with a pack of God-knows-what closing in on us?"

Fair question, and he had to admit, while the one he had his eye on hadn't moved again, it did sound like the others were getting closer. Footsteps rustled somewhere out there. Or maybe raw panic was sharpening his sense of hearing. Fear had a way of doing that.

"All right, I'll countdown, we're going to take three steps in your direction. We'll see what they do. Keep your gun on the one that's right there," Gordon said.

As if Richard needed to be told not to lower his weapon.

The plan didn't sound all that strong, but he couldn't come up with anything better, and Gordon was already saying, "Three."

Richard trained the barrel of his gun on the spot between the monster's eyes.

"Two."

His finger itched on the trigger.

"One."

Twin red lights sliced through the dark. The cacophony of rapid gunfire sliced through the relative quiet. Gordon slammed into him, knocking him to the ground. His pistol flew out of his hand and clattered away into a tangle of fallen branches. Lying on his back, he saw a small orb catch the light from his phone and reflect it back. A moment later, the object landed with a soft thud and exploded. A mushroom cloud of purple smoke rolled twenty feet up into the air and slammed back to earth, creating a pressure wave that blew in Richard's face like a hurricane. Gordon lay over Richard, protecting him from the battle until the explosive noise died away and the dust, quite literally, settled again.

"You okay?" Gordon asked.

"I think you might have broke one of my ribs."

"Sorry, instincts."

Richard harrumphed and hauled himself into a sitting position to find himself on his butt with his legs splayed out in front of him for the second time that night.

"Who's there?" he called out.

He'd dropped his gun but somehow kept a hand on his phone. He shined it toward the spot where the shots had originated. The light caught the shiny dome of Stan Kapcheck's head as he and Burke emerged from the thicket where they'd taken cover.

"Thought you chaps might need a hand." Friggin' Stan Kapcheck grinned like a fool at his wedding.

"We wouldn't have needed a thing if you hadn't sent us out here in the middle of nowhere with no information and then run off to wherever it is you've been," Richard grumbled.

Stanley offered a hand, and after a moment's hesitation, Richard took it and allowed himself to be yanked up onto his feet.

"My apologies. In retrospect, I see I should have shared more details," Stanley said.

"Even just a few might have been helpful."

"Touché," Stanley said in typical weirdo fashion.

Gordon already had his arms around Burke. "Thanks for saving our skin."

She grinned. "It's what we do."

"We thought you got rid of us on purpose so we could come out here and save you if things went sideways," Gordon said, one arm around Burke.

Stanley rummaged in his bag and came up with a flashlight as long as his arm. "I did."

"Good thing we did such a bang-up job," Richard muttered.

"Things have a way of working out the way they're supposed to." Stanley strolled to the edge of the crater and shined his light across the blasted expanse. His head shook subtly from side to side as if he'd recently developed palsy. "This can't be."

Richard spotted his walking stick on the ground and stooped to pick it up. His back hurt, his hip was hitching, and his bones were dang-near frozen with the weird damp cold that never seemed to let up in this god-forsaken place. A good sturdy stick would come in handy if he had to haul his tired old body two miles back to the cabin. Leaning heavily on the aid, he told Stanley that the hole hadn't been there when we arrived.

"You almost would have—"

Stanley held a hand up for silence. He cocked his head, listening for a moment, and then took off toward the tree line.

"Let's talk about it back at the cabin," he said without making eye contact with anyone. Those things we just killed are maybe the least awful thing that stalks this forest at night."

That plan was just peachy by Richard's standards. A warm, dry cabin with a decent bed and a hot shower was exactly where he wanted to be.

CHAPTER TWENTY-TWO

Burke

THE HOT SHOWER THREATENED TO MELT THE SKIN OFF Burke's bones. Come hell or high water, she would wash away the night in the forest, the memory of trudging through the valley of bones, and the close call with Gordon and her grandfather. How long would they have been able to hold those creatures off? It was a miracle they hadn't already been torn to bits.

At last, the cabin's tank ran dry, and the stream cooled. She stepped out, toweled herself as dry as possible in the tiny, steam-filled room, and wrestled her body into a pair of sweats and her favorite fuzzy socks. Tylenol kept her functional, but when she emerged and found the three men seated around the table, she announced they had one hour before she took the other stuff to knock her out.

"Fair enough. We all need to rest and be sharp. We've lost too much time on this investigation already." Stanley wrapped his hands around his cup of tea but made no move to drink it. "I suspect we've all learned a great deal."

"I'll go first since you just about got us killed twice over by sending us into an unknown situation." Richard produced a leather-wrapped bundle and laid it on the table, pushing it forward with the tips of his fingers, as if loathe to make contact.

"When we arrived at the coordinates you indicated, there was a circle where everything had been destroyed," Gordon explained.

"Unhallowed ground?" Stanley frowned. "That wouldn't make sense."

"Sort of, but different," Richard explained. "We figured out it was a door."

"How? I wouldn't have had any idea where to begin if I came across something like that."

Pink spots bloomed on Richard's cheeks. "When I stepped into it, it opened."

Stanley drew back. "Why would you step into a circle of unhallowed ground?"

"Well, as you pointed out, it wasn't unhallowed ground," Richard shot back before taking an intense interest in the cheese squares on the plate in front of him. "Besides, I didn't mean to. I just...it...these things happen sometimes."

"I see," Stanley said.

Burke gave him points for his visible effort to contain his amusement. It wasn't the first time Richard quite literally stumbled into danger. He had a knack for it.

"And what happened when the door opened?" Stanley asked.

"The weirdest thing I ever saw." Richard shook a finger in Stanley's direction. "And I've seen some weird things."

Stanley didn't argue. "No doubt, my friend."

"Soon as I stepped in that circle, a ghost came out."

Burke kept her eyes on Stanley.

He steepled his fingers under his chin. "The veil was thin. I wondered about that possibility."

Richard shook his head. "It wasn't your regular run-of-the-mill ghost, though. It was a monster ghost."

A smile played on Stan's lips. "That's not possible."

"Reevaluate your definition of possible," Gordon said.

They all turned to him, and he shrugged. "Sure as shit looked like monster ghosts to me."

"'Ghosts'?" Stanley asked. "More than one?"

Richard blew out an enormous exhale, letting his lips flap together like a tired horse. "Yes, Stan. More than one. Dozens. Hundreds. Maybe more. Legions. Friggin' ghost soup. Every one of them with teeth and claws and all the monster stuff."

Stanley continued to argue. "Monsters have no souls. When we kill them, they go back to the nothing from which they came. They're not like humans."

"Maybe they're more like us than you think," Gordon suggested.

A wild mix of emotions flitted across Stanley's face. He blinked hard and gave himself a little shake. "Okay. Putting that aside for later, please continue."

"We drew a salt line, and that held them, and then I cast a locking spell," Richard said.

Faced with the same situation, Burke doubted she'd have had the presence of mind to come up with a solution as neat and simple. "Well done, Grandpa."

He scowled. "Someday, you're going to realize I ain't just a stupid old man."

"I never...." She sighed. He was even crankier than usual, and she was too tired to navigate that minefield. She let it drop and sent a silent prayer of thanks when he did the same.

"The locking spell did something, though. It went off like a bomb." He jerked a thumb in Gordon's direction. "Knocked old special forces here right on his keister. When the smoke cleared, poof, no more ghosts."

"The crater we saw, that was from the spell?" Burke thought

of the scooped-out hole she'd seen. She'd never seen magic with that level of violence and strength. The idea turned her recently boiled bones chilly once more.

"It was, and in the middle, Gordon found that." Richard gestured toward the bundle on the table. "I don't know what it is, but I knew enough not to touch it."

For a long moment, they all sat there staring at the bundle. At last, Stanley reached out and pulled it close. He unfolded the first flap, the second, and the third, then stopped and looked around the table. Finally, he uncovered the object.

"Gordon and I reckon those are aliens." Richard's dentures clicked as he pushed them around his mouth.

"Perhaps you're right," Stanley said. The ancient called them gods. Who are we to say?"

"What is it?" Gordon leaned over the table for a closer look. "When I first picked it up, I thought bone or ivory, but in this light, I'm not so sure."

"It's a tooth," Stanley explained.

Richard joined Gordon in close examination. "Paint me green and call me a pickle, but what in the Sam Hill has teeth that big?" Richard blurted.

"I don't know, but thousands of years ago, someone hunted a creature that did. The hunter then inscribed these symbols and"—Stanley held up a hand in a gesture that admitted he was at a loss—"somehow, they managed to create the most powerful totem I've ever encountered or even heard of."

A shiver skittered over the surface of Burke's skin. Stanley once told them he first became a hunter when he encountered a magical totem by accident. He'd picked it up and, while holding it in his hand, he could control every living thing around him— even to the point of commanding them to die. Whatever *this* thing was, he considered it more powerful than the other.

"Some things aren't meant to be in human hands." She hadn't meant to say it out loud, but there it was.

"Indeed." Stanley recovered the enormous tooth and slid it back toward the center of the table. "I saw this object destroyed when Busar used it." He rubbed his fingers over his mouth before continuing. "Not just broken, but obliterated, disintegrated, turned to dust."

"Yet here it is." Burke's concepts of magic were being pushed past anything she'd conceived of prior to this strange and exhausting adventure.

Stanley's gaze remained fixed on the leather bundle. "Yes, here it is."

"Should we try to use it again?" Gordon asked.

"No!" The other three shouted in unison.

Stanley ran a hand over his head. "I think we would do best, for now, to lock it in a warded box." He took a deep breath. "And speaking of warding, we've been lax. Whoever put the hex bag on the porch possesses considerable skill. Transporting two people is not amateur magic."

"You want us to ward the cabin?" The idea of painting runes just then made Burke want to crawl under the table and hide.

Stanley rose and came around the table to rest a gentle hand on her uninjured shoulder. "I'll do it. You've been more than brave. Rest. Richard will help me."

Her grandfather grunted but rose without saying anything and plodded out to the car to find a can of paint.

"I'll get food," Gordon said. "If we've still got work to do, we need some decent nourishment."

He dashed off and returned faster than she dreamed possible, carrying bags full of groceries. She spotted a Styrofoam tray of pork chops and a microwavable bowl of macaroni and cheese. A rolled-up newspaper peeked over the top of one of the bags.

"That little store in the lobby has a surprisingly decent stock for a tiny place in the middle of nowhere."

From where he worked by the window, Richard shared his

thoughts. "If they sold poop and moldy bread, it would be a step up from that hoity-toity joke of a place we went to last night."

Protected from outside magic, sitting behind plates laden with hot food, they gathered around the table again. Gordon laid his cards out for all of them to see.

Stanley started them off. "Before you explain what these all mean, it would be prudent of me to share with you what Burke and I discovered."

Burke used the edge of her fork to form her macaroni into a perfect patty shape. This was Stanley's business to tell, not hers.

"The place where we were sent was familiar to me. Last time I was here, Busar and I discovered it. There is a clan of dryads who've created a sort of magical force field around a portion of the forest. It's not the kind of magic that can't be overcome, but anyone who goes within the boundaries they've set will experience a near overwhelming sense of fear and unease. Their every instinct will scream at them to leave."

Burke could affirm the truth of his statement.

"Within the dryad territory, we found a cave. Busar and I speculated that perhaps if we were able to bind and transport the boogeyman, we could contain him within that cave. It was far too sturdy for a physical being to break out of, and the dryad warding would all but eliminate the possibility of some unfortunate soul stumbling across the creature." Stanley cut off a small bite of pork and chewed it carefully before going on.

"Burke and I left the cabin with the intention of hiking to the coordinates I sent you, but the moment we stepped past the hex bag, we found ourselves at the border of the warded land. Of course, it would have been all but impossible to use magic to cross the warding."

Burke poked a hole in the middle of her cheesy creation. She peeked over at her grandfather. He'd almost cleaned his plate already. How could anyone eat that fast with no real teeth?

"My instincts told me to find the cave, so that's what we did." Stanley cut, chewed, and swallowed another forkful. "Busar was there."

Richard's fork clattered against his plate. "You found him?"

"We did," Stanley confirmed.

Richard prompted him to continue. "And? Drop the other shoe, man."

"And he can't possibly be our killer. He's been locked away for thirteen years. Busar is not killing the children."

Gordon reached into his breast pocket, produced his note-cards, and spread them on the table. "That fits with what we learned. Busar was seen around the area on a regular basis until about that time. Then he disappeared without a word to anyone, so far as we found."

Pointing at a card that caught her eye, Burke asked, "What is this about?"

"The ME is a ghoul," Gordon explained.

"Yes, I see that's what it says, but can you elaborate on your encounter with the ghoul?"

"He was ugly." Richard scraped the last bits of cheese sauce from his plate and popped the spoon into his mouth.

"We had no idea until we went to his office, but he made no effort to hide it from us. He knew before we showed up that we were hunters."

Stanley folded his arms over his chest. "That explains why he was so quick to accept the appointment. Usually, there's some posturing involved in setting those meetings up, but he agreed immediately when I asked."

"How did he know?" The idea that some*thing* had followed them into town, knew who they were, and had been toying with them all along sank roots into the fertile soil of Burke's mind.

"He said the current situation is similar to what happened before, so he expected hunters, but it's not the same. These kids are dying too fast," Gordon said.

Richard pushed his empty plate aside and rubbed his belly like a pregnant woman soothing an unborn baby kicking her in the ribs. "He's also the one who helped us figure out the two of you fell in a trap."

"I see," Stanley said. "A most helpful ghoul, indeed."

"Don't it bother you to know that a monster's working at the county building?"

"Not at all, my friend. I told you, this part of the world is unique. The monsters have integrated to an astonishing degree. A ghoul does not eat the flesh of the living. It sounds like he has a steady food supply. I've not heard of a mass turning in this area. He's doing no harm. There are many others. Look with careful eyes when you interact with the locals, and you'll see what I mean."

"That reminds me"—Gordon leaned forward and fished through the cards until his hand landed upon one in particular—"we met a lady who was eager to see you, Stan. She was...." He floundered, apparently uncertain how to describe the woman.

"Electric. Like an eel," Richard said.

To Burke's surprise, Gordon agreed that it was an apt description. He pushed the card toward Stanley, who reached out and accepted it with the gentle care of a man holding a newborn chick.

"Loretta." The word, coming from Stanley's lips, had the reverent quality of a prayer. In his hand, the notecard shook. He set it on the table and folded his fingers together.

The curiosity was too much for Burke to withstand. "Who is she?"

"She's...we.... Her...I...." Stanley cleared his throat and swallowed hard. "Loretta and I were close, a long time ago, but she is not why we're here. Let's stay on topic."

While Burke was still concocting all sorts of wild, romantic, violent, terrifying, and glorious scenarios around Stanley and the mysterious, electric Loretta, Richard moved on to the next subject.

"You ought to add a card for the witch. We ain't got the foggiest who it might be, but we know it's someone powerful enough to blast two hunters from here to the Canadian border. Could be magic like that draws on the life force of the kids around here."

Stanley's brows shot up. "That's a fantastically astute observation, Dick."

Richard scowled. "Not sure why everybody's always so surprised when I have a good idea. I might not be as fast as the other kids, but I get to the park eventually."

Circling back to their unfortunate, unplanned trip into the heart of the forest prompted a question in Burke's mind. "Why did the witch send us to that place? I mean, no way it was coincidence. We could have spent a lifetime wandering in that wilderness and never come upon Busar. Why were we sent to him?"

"Why not killed?" Richard asked. "Magic like that, they could have turned your guts inside out before you had time to know what was happening."

A fresh zing of energy zipped through Burke's core. "You're right. That's bigger magic that we encounter on any kind of regular basis. As big as what we saw the leprechaun do, maybe."

Richard stuck his finger in his ear and poked around at his hearing aid. "And if the leprechaun patched up Stan, maybe this witch has enough juice to patch Busar."

Burke expected an argument from Stanley, but it never came. Instead, he sagged, looking like an old man for once. "I don't know if that can be done. I seriously doubt it, but you all should know, I had a lot of time to think while we walked. I won't leave Busar again. If that means I live out my days on this peninsula, then you'll move on without me."

All three of them shifted, and Stanley raised a hand. "I won't hear a word otherwise. I've made up my mind. I can't live with myself any other way. I shouldn't have left him in the first place. He would never have left me if he'd had a choice. I was scared, and I acted like a child. I won't do it again."

Burke laid a hand on his forearm. "Then we have that much motivation to be sure he can be healed."

"First things first, though." Gordon stood and fetched the newspaper, folded back to page five, and laid it in the center of the table. "We don't have time to get sidetracked. The death count is up to five, and two more kids are sick."

They spent another hour rehashing facts and getting nowhere. The boost in Burke's energy died down, leaving her even more exhausted. She caved into her body's demands, took one of the more powerful painkillers, and excused herself to go to bed. Before she closed the door, she heard the men agree that they shouldn't leave themselves vulnerable with so many unknowns. Gordon agreed to take the first watch.

CHAPTER TWENTY-THREE

Richard

RICHARD WOKE UP FEELING SO BATTERED AND BANGED UP,
part of him wished he'd died in the night. He'd be tempted to
deal with The Devil if she showed up just then with a nice big
tin of that balm that enchanted all the aches and pains away. As
it was, he'd have to make do with aspirin and willpower.

On his way to the kitchen, he shuffled like the old man he
seldom felt like anymore. Picking his feet up required more
effort than he could muster up. Stanley sat at the table in black
slacks and a cashmere sweater. What kind of hunter packed
cashmere sweaters in his duffle? Gordon's ever-present note-
cards lay scattered across the wooden tabletop.

"Good morning, Dick."

Richard made it to the coffee pot. "You been up long?"

"A few hours. I woke and couldn't settle down, so I figured
I'd relieve Gordon."

"No sign of Burke?"

"Still sleeping, as far as I know."

The water hissed inside the machine, and the strong black

brew dripped out. While he waited, Richard got the prune juice and poured himself a nice, tall glass. It wouldn't do to get his guts all tied up in the middle of a big hunt like this one.

"You think she's okay? This bum shoulder's getting to her more than she lets on, I think."

"Agreed, my friend, but I think time will heal this wound, and she'll be back to her usual self before we know it. For now, rest is the best thing for her, and under the influence of those painkillers, I imagine she'll sleep a few more hours."

It only took a few minutes to whip up two slices of peanut butter toast. By the time he was done, the coffee finished brewing. Richard took his breakfast to the table and sat in the chair to Stanley's right. He pointed at the card with Loretta's name on it. Stanley moved it to a place of honor, front and center.

"Spill the beans. Who's the good-looking broad with the pretty eyes and the tight sweater? And don't be feeding me some kind of hogwash about how that's a story for another day. We're old men. We might not have too many other days."

Stanley traced the letters of the woman's name with his forefinger. "She's an angel."

"Well, I could tell right away, she wasn't your average Susie Q. She's the kind of dame a man remembers."

Stanley chuckled. "I can't argue with any of that, but you're not understanding what I'm telling you. Loretta is an angel—an actual, literal angel from Heaven."

Stanley often took a sick joy in yanking Richard's chain. Richard chewed his toast with slow deliberation, trying to decide the best course to follow with this conversation to avoid looking like a donkey's hind end.

Stanley laughed again. "You don't believe me?"

"I ain't decided yet," Richard told him. "In all this time, you ain't never once mentioned that angels are real."

"I never told you they weren't."

Richard scratched his head.

"Come now." Stanley leaned back and crossed his arms. "You've met The Devil Herself. If she's real, and the place from which she comes is real, why would her opposite not be real?"

"I ain't never doubted the existence of God," Richard said, and that was true. He wasn't always sure of his own personal status with The Creator, but he believed.

"God is not The Devil's opposite," Stanley said. "You're giving her far too much credit. She's not omnipotent. You've seen her defeated twice in less than a year."

Another bite of his toast bought Richard a moment to think about that. It was true that they'd beat The Devil, but it had been a close thing both times, and he'd not be quick to pick a fight with her again.

"What does your Bible tell you about The Devil and her demons?" Stanley asked.

From time to time, Stanley slipped into this pedantic mode. For the most part, Richard accepted it. Stanley was annoying as a bad case of crabs, but there was no denying he knew a good many things that Richard did not.

"They were all angels, once upon a time," Richard said.

"That was a long, long time ago, but that is, indeed, how it began."

The hot coffee was the perfect counter to the sticky sweetness of the peanut butter. He could practically hear his neurons squeaking like rusty hinges on an old screen door while he tried to assimilate the lovely Loretta into his worldview.

Stanley raised an eyebrow. "You've expressed a belief in the Christian faith, yet when shown evidence that you're right, you act as though you never knew such a thing could be."

But Richard wasn't thinking about his religious beliefs just then. "You...she...I mean.... The Devil and an angel? That's just...."

He lacked a word for how he felt about the fact that Stanley had bedded not just half the mortals in the world but at least one being from both Heaven and Hell. Who else? Did he ever make it with a little green alien? Probably. Friggin' Stan Kapcheck.

"She and I shared a brief but lovely time together. I'm afraid, however, that, in my distress over the situation with Busar, I did not give her the attention that was due to her. Still, I like to believe we left on good terms. She understood that the way it was, was the way it needed to be."

A lightbulb popped on in Richard's mind, shining so bright he barely registered what Stanley said about his failed relationship with the angel. "Hey! She must have some kind of powers, right? I mean, The Devil could snap her fingers, teleport, and blow ghosts to dust and all sorts of things. You should call her up and ask her to help us. If she's an angel, she's going to want to help the kids, right? Isn't that the kind of business she's in?"

Stanley rubbed a hand over his bald head. "No. She's an angel, not one of the fallen, but she's chosen to live on Earth as an observer. She cannot interfere. It's forbidden. If she uses Heavenly magic among the mortals, she'll face serious consequences."

"You told me to think about the Bible stories. Angels interfered all the time in the Bible, the way I remember it."

"Perhaps," Stanley conceded. "But never of their own volition. There is a significant difference between acting on the orders of God and choosing to intervene in human affairs with celestial magic."

Deflated, Richard slumped over his plate. His sweet Barbara would have chided him for having his elbows on the table, but just then, his old bones required a bit of extra support. When Stanley had been in town before, he'd been on a job, but that hadn't stopped him from meeting a pretty girl or—

Richard slapped a knobby-knuckled hand on the table. "There was a guy outside the police station. Ray. He knew you." Lord help him; if Stanley admitted going to bed with that guy, too, Richard was going to toss his cookies right there on the table.

Thankfully, Stanley only laughed. "Ray, you say? That's got to be Raven. Now there's an interesting character for you, and one your Bible does not mention, though it probably should have. Geographical limitations, I suppose. Raven's always hung around this continent, so he wouldn't have been part of old Abraham's world."

"He's a monster?"

Stan's head bobbed from side to side like a cockatoo's. "Not so much. I mean, he doesn't eat humans or turn people."

"He's not human, though."

"Oh, no, definitely not human," Stanley said. "I'd put him more in the category of a demigod, though he's not exactly that, either. He's a trickster, rather like Loki."

"Loki. The guy from that comic book movie?"

"Dick, I'm delighted at your modern movie knowledge. Yes, one in the same, though the movie took some significant liberties."

Richard pressed his thumb against the crumbs on his plate and licked them off. "Well, I ain't been living under a rock, if that's what you mean, but wasn't Loki the bad guy?"

"Significant liberties," Stanley repeated. "Anyway, I have no idea where Loki is, or if he's still alive. I am delighted to hear about Raven, though."

"You think he'll be helpful?"

Stanley laughed like Richard just dropped the punchline of some fantastic joke. "Oh, no. He will not be helpful. He's not to be trusted. His life's work and deepest joy is to create mischief. He's not evil, though. I've never known him to cause true harm and, occasionally, if the spirit moves him, he'll do something nice for a human who's found favor with him."

Toast gone and coffee cup emptied, the right thing to do would be to take his dishes to the sink and wash them, but his old bones pleaded with him to take a break and be still, so he obliged and let his gaze wander over Gordon's notecards.

Ray was missing from the collection of names and facts. Probably, like Richard, Gordon had dismissed him as a random background character in the story of whatever was going on in the area. If he knew Stanley, though, and if he had a thing for playing tricks, they should add him. Magicking two people into the middle of the forest was a pretty good trick. Under other circumstances, Richard might even have found it amusing.

Loretta was an angel. How did Stanley find these women? And what was so special about him that an angel and The Devil Herself both fell for him? Some questions had no answers.

The ME ghoul was one of the monsters on their side so far as they could tell, just like the preacher thing that gave Stan and Burke a lift home.

Strange times had descended upon them when half the job was working with the monsters instead of hunting them. Still, if there were enough of them, just maybe....

"Do you think we could get all the friendly spooks to help out?"

Stanley fiddled with Loretta's card. "Maybe, but first, we have to figure out what we need help with. At this point, the only thing we've succeeded in is raising questions. If we don't know what's killing these kids, how can we fight it?"

Richard looked at the card closest to him, one that Gordon must have altered during the night:

~~2~~ dead ~~3~~ 5

"We've got to be quick about it."

CHAPTER TWENTY-FOUR

Burke

WRAPPED IN A QUILT, SITTING IN ONE OF THE ROCKING chairs on the cabin's porch, Burke wondered at the anxiety this land provoked in her. Rain fell on the rolling, white-capped ocean waves in great silvery sheets. The sound brought to mind the soothing meditation CDs so often sold in new-age shops. Why then, did it grate on her nerves rather than soothe them?

She turned her attention to the blackened circle on the floor, the remains of the hex bag. "It's not weird to feel anxious when someone really is out to get you."

The screen door opened with a screech of rusty hinges and Gordon stepped out. "Talking to someone?"

"Having a conversation with the voices in my head."

"Sometimes that's the only place a person can find a decent conversationalist." He gestured at the empty chair beside her. "Do you mind some company?"

"Your company is always welcome." It took her a while to figure that out, but now that she knew, she was confident in her statement.

For a time, they rocked side-by-side in comfortable silence.

"This place is so immense in every way; it makes me feel small and weak as a child," Gordon said.

"Same."

A pickup truck, sans muffler, roared by on the twisting road beyond the office building/store. Burke was grateful for the reminder that other people still existed somewhere. This place may just be too remote, too lonely. She'd never last if she was ever sent to one of those arctic exploration stations.

With her right foot, she pointed toward the burn marks. "I've been thinking about that."

"Do tell," Gordon said.

Was she ready to put this thought into words? Her consciousness was circling around something, but whatever that central nugget of truth was, she'd yet to latch onto it.

"Witches are human."

"Okay."

The chairs creaked against the planks, a sound that blended with the infinite susurration of the sea.

"Well, monsters are pretty easy to understand, most of the time," she continued. "They're driven by their appetites and by their desire to reproduce."

"Aren't we all?"

She stuck her tongue out at him and was rewarded with a rare smile. "Fine, but the question is, why does a witch do what they do?"

"Why does anyone follow any religion?"

"I'm not talking about Wiccans or people who worship the trees or whatever. I'm talking about the kinds of witches who play with powers humans were never meant to touch."

Gordon stretched his long legs out and crossed his ankles. "No offense intended, but I've seen you and your little posse fiddle with some of those kinds of powers. Whatever Richard did the other night was far outside the scope of natural. If we'd been in the city, he could have taken out the better part of a block with that one spell."

"That was because of the totem, I think. Normally, a spell like that—" He raised an eyebrow and realized she answered her own question. "Okay. We use witchcraft, rarely, to fight monsters. I still say that's not the same thing as crafting hex bags and cursing our enemies."

"No, I suppose it's not."

"So, if a person isn't using magic to fight magic, why would they use it?"

"Power? It must be quite a rush to believe you can manipulate reality to your will."

She shrugged. "I suppose."

A gull circled over the ocean. If she sat in this place ten thousand years ago, would it look any different? Doubtful.

Gordon's chair squeaked when he planted his feet and leaned his elbows on his knees. "I think the question you're trying to ask is, what purpose did this particular spell serve? Why would someone send you to Busar?"

"Exactly. What did they achieve by doing that?"

"Maybe they hoped he would kill you," Gordon said.

"But if they had enough power and skill to send us away, killing us would have been simple."

"We're guessing. Maybe they wanted this, maybe they acted because of that. Let's look at the known. What did they achieve? What is different now because of that hex bag?"

Phrased like that, it couldn't have been more obvious. "Now we know that Busar is alive and that he's innocent."

"How does that change your investigation?" he asked.

"At the moment, knowing he isn't the killer has stopped it altogether. We don't know which way to turn, so we're just sort of wandering vaguely around and not accomplishing much."

Gordon nodded. "It does feel that way. We should be in motion. Those children need help sooner rather than later."

"I agree, but motion for motion's sake is a waste of energy. If this was your case, back on the cruise ship, what would you do?"

He didn't hesitate with his answer. "I'd talk to the victims of the crime or those who were with them at the time, and I'd do it face-to-face. No phone calls. No warning that I was coming. I'd want to see their reactions without giving them time to prepare or fix up a story first."

"You have their addresses in those files you got?" she asked.

"I do."

"Then I guess it's time to get in motion again."

She stood.

An explosion inside the cabin shook the building.

CHAPTER TWENTY-FIVE

Richard

GORDON AND BURKE BURST THROUGH THE DOOR LIKE A SWAT team landing on top of the Mafia.

"Everything's fine," Stanley reassured them.

Nevertheless, the lovebirds hustled like a couple of cats with their tails on fire to join Richard and Stanley in the little sitting area. Stanley rolled back the rug and moved the coffee table aside. They drew a salt line and set the totem in the center of it.

Burke squatted like a frog at the edge of the salt line. "What happened?"

"Absolutely nothing; therein lies the mystery." Stanley flipped through the pages of a book, not looking up while he answered her. "I cast a revelation spell, and it ricocheted."

Her gaze traveled to the place on the wall where black scorch marks indicated the energy's exit point. Heat rose to Richard's cheeks. The revelation spell had been his idea. One time outside of Tulsa, they'd found a crystal of suspect origins. A revelation spell forced the thing to play out its past like a poorly projected movie, and they learned it had been used to trap a demon. Knowing that allowed them to dispose of the object in an appropriate manner.

"It was a good idea," Stanley said as if he could read Richard's mind. "Starting with the simplest spell and working your way up is a method that shows both wisdom and prudence."

Burke rose to her full height with impressive ease. Her knees didn't even pop. "Who are you trying to convince?"

Stanley turned another page in his book. Richard kept his mouth shut. Better to be thought a fool than to say something stupid and confirm it.

"Burke and I were thinking about going into town to talk to the families of the victims. We hate to dredge up their pain, but we're getting nowhere fast, and the clock is ticking for those kids." Gordon kept his eye on the totem while he spoke.

Everyone agreed it was the best course of action.

"Dick and I will stay here," Stanley said. "I didn't ask as many questions as I should have when Busar and I used this before. It's impossible to know exactly what magical properties something so ancient possesses, but the fact that it healed itself is extraordinary. I'd like to learn as much as I can."

"We could ask Busar," Burke suggested.

Stanley twitched. Maybe he had a sudden itch. Maybe it was something much more significant. Hard to tell with Stan Kapcheck. "I'd rather not. Keep in touch, please. It would be best if none of us ended up out in the woods again."

Richard and Stanley spent the next quarter of an hour skimming the pages of the magic books. In his imagination, behind the sounds of Gordon and Burke dressing and saying goodbye, the tires of the car grinding across the gravel drive, the distant rolling of the sea, and the rain falling on the roof, he heard a clock ticking. The kid was right. They were moving too slow. They needed to take action, and they needed to do it quickly, but what to do? And do it to whom?

"I'm going to try this." Stanley turned his book toward Richard.

The text was in Latin, so Richard could only make out about every fifth word, but he saw "revelare" at least five times. "It's another revealing spell, isn't it?"

"It's older than the other and uses earth magic rather than fire magic." Richard harrumphed. "I'm sure that will make all the difference. We'll open a crack in the Earth and fall into the abyss instead of nearly burning the cabin down."

"It's been a good run," Stanley said with a twinkle in his eye.

No arguing with that.

Another ten minutes ticked by while they gathered what they needed and arranged it all within arm's reach.

"What happens if this one ricochets?" Richard wondered aloud.

"You hold on to your butt," Stanley replied unreassuringly.

Stanley drew the symbols on the wooden floor with a white teacher's chalk. He pressed both palms to the center of his creation and began speaking in a tongue Richard couldn't name. The glasses in the cabinet clinked together, making a sound like fairy chatter, when the cabin trembled as if nervous. Richard didn't blame the old building. He was nervous, too.

At last, the chanting paused, and Richard poured the bowl of earth they'd collected over Stanley's hands. The lights flickered and went out, leaving only the gloom of the stormy day. Five rays grew like long, straight, brown snakes emerging from their holes and slithering in opposite directions. Each shimmered as if made from dust mixed with silvery glitter.

Richard scooted back on his chair and surreptitiously slid his hands under the seat of his pants. The first ray bumped into the wooden dining table and reduced it to dust. Another slipped under the door. From outside, wood creaked and the land shook when a giant tree fell across the driveway with an astounding thud. The third ray touched a window and dissolved, leaving behind the wet scent of leaf mold and freshly turned dirt. The fourth and the fifth stopped growing and hovered in the air.

One of the rays took shape. It grew arms and legs, a powerfully muscled form. A severe face with a broad nose and high cheekbones looked out from behind a shimmering brown screen, searching but not seeing the two men. With his long arms, he reached out, feeling around him like a blind man. He took a hesitant step forward and then another but managed to go nowhere.

The last ray spiraled around the ghostly image, creating a web that closed in tighter and tighter. The man, or the thing that looked like a man, appeared to be oblivious to his capture. He simply went on searching.

With a grunt that sounded like something from a wounded water buffalo, Stanley wrenched his hands away from the spellwork. The scene before them crashed to the floor, sending up a plume of dust that left both men coughing and sputtering for the next two minutes.

Richard wiped the dust from his face. His mouth tasted of dirt. "Explain."

"Earth magic, my friend, amplified magnificently."

"Magnificent?" Richard harrumphed again. "Any thoughts about the naked dude behind the veil."

"Several." Stanley walked to the sink and splashed water on his face.

"You inclined to share those thoughts?"

After drying his face and hands on a small blue kitchen towel, Stanley propped one hip against the counter. "It appeared to be Busar."

"Well, what in the name of St. Pete's hamster was he doing in there?"

Stanley's eyes twinkled. He looked happier than he had in quite some time. "He appeared to be searching for a way out."

CHAPTER TWENTY-SIX

Burke

JOSEPH AND WANDA SMITHFIELD LIVED IN A SINGLE-STORY brick home dwarfed by the three enormous barns forming a semi-circle around the house. The entire lot had been clear-cut, so it stood out like an alien desert amid the lush green growth that surrounded it on every side. Gordon stopped the Cadillac near the front porch, uncertain where else to park as there were no marked areas, only a large patch of hard-packed earth. To get there, they'd had to bounce and bump a mile and a half down a dirt path that resembled a donkey trail more than a modern road.

Burke took the lead, standing slightly in front of Gordon and knocking on the door.

The woman who answered was a natural beauty, tiny, slim, fit, with blond curls and big blue eyes. But dark circles stole the glimmer from her pretty eyes. Her posture sagged as if she were carrying an enormous weight and had been for far too long.

Guilt plowed through Burke's belly. No part of her wanted to drag this poor woman through her raw, painful memories.

But what else could they do? How many more mothers would suffer her fate if the hunters failed?

Burke didn't smile. This wasn't a happy occasion. Rather, she tried to inject every ounce of sympathy into her voice. After confirming that she was speaking with Wanda Smithfield, Burke introduced herself and Gordon. "I'm Agent Martin. This is my associate, Agent Westchester." They flashed the fake badges Stanley had made. "We're very sorry to bother you, but we have some questions about your son."

Wanda's brow furrowed. "Did they find something with one of the other kids? Is that why the CDC is involved. I've got three other little ones."

"I'm afraid we are still looking for answers," Burke said. "With what we know at this time, we have no reason to believe your other children are in any danger. We're just looking for links, any small thing that might connect the children who've gotten sick."

The woman held the door with one hand and the frame with the other as though she might collapse if she let go. Her gaze wandered toward Gordon and meandered back to Burke again, and Burke wondered if she had been prescribed something a little on the strong side to help her handle her grief.

"May we come in? We won't take long."

"Joe's not home right now. He went to Port Angeles to pick up parts for the air compressor."

"That's okay. If we need to, we can come back some other time to talk to him."

Wanda turned and went back inside, leaving the door open. Burke and Gordon followed her, despite the lack of a formal invitation.

Toys and clothes cluttered every surface, but a thin film of dust topped the baseboards and the bookshelves. Only recently had housekeeping been neglected. Burke didn't judge the other woman in the slightest. How did a person find the motivation to care about dust when their child had been torn from their life? It was impressive she'd even managed to get herself out of bed and get dressed, let alone care for three other children.

They sat in the living room. Wanda chewed on her fingernails while she waited for them to ask their questions.

"Your son, Lucas, he was six years old?" Burke already knew that information from reading the files Gordon had picked up, but she figured it was best to start with the simple stuff. It might get Wanda talking, and there was never any telling what might prompt a person to say what they needed to hear to link all the pieces together.

"He would have been seven in the spring. He kept telling us he wanted an archaeology party. Joe was going to build a whole setup with the sandbox and shark's teeth and costume jewelry buried out there. It would have kept Lucas busy all summer."

"Was he in school?"

Wanda nodded. "First grade."

"Did you notice anything strange around the time he got sick, anything at all," Burke asked. "It could have been something he said or something environmental. A strange smell? Cold spots? Was he having nightmares or sleepwalking?"

She shook her head. "No. He was fine, always the healthiest one in the house. Last year, when everybody got sick, he was the only one in the family that got passed right over."

Gordon produced a little notepad from his pocket and made a note. "Did your son have any friends—children or adults—outside the family that he spent a great deal of time with?"

Picking at her ragged nails, Wanda shrugged. "I mean, we went to church, and he was in a class there with some kids he liked to play with, and he had friends at school. Sometimes they'd sleep over here, or he'd go there. He loved art. Last summer, he took a class with his little buddy JR at the children's art center in Forks. Nothing out of the ordinary."

"Where do you go to church?" Gordon asked.

"Calvary Chapel." She rubbed the back of her neck.

"In case there's anything environmental, would you mind if we looked around? We'd especially like to see where Lucas slept."

"It's a mess in there. I haven't been after the other kids like I should clean it up."

Gordon gave her a gentle smile. "Don't worry about any of that. We understand, but if there're any clues at all, we'd like to find them as soon as possible."

Wanda's voice sounded small and frightened as a child's when she said, "How many kids, now?"

Burke almost hated to say the word. It felt like an indictment. They were moving too slow. She swallowed hard and forced it past her lips. "Seven."

"Seven?" Wanda repeated. Tears welled in her eyes. "The kids all share a room. It's back here."

She led them through the kitchen to a large room that had obviously been added to the main structure as an afterthought. It was a child's dream—two sets of bunk beds beneath a ceiling painted to look like a starry sky. A swing hung from a sturdy metal stand in the center of the room. Shelves that held bins of Lego bricks, action figures, toy cars, and picture books covered the walls. Clearly, the other three children tossed items aside and left them wherever they landed. The beds were unmade with covers hanging off or bunched up at the foot, except for one.

The top bunk on the left side of the room was neatly made with a Star Wars comforter spread over it and a toy Yoda doll lying with its head on the pillow. The last time Lucas left the bed, Wanda had made it up for him in anticipation of his return, but he'd never come home.

When Gordon spoke up, Wanda blinked back. He pointed at a five-by-seven photograph in a frame on the wall next to Lucas's bed. The little blond-haired boy stood beside an attractive older woman with her arm around him. He proudly displayed a simple but well-executed drawing of a dinosaur. "Who's this?"

"That's the teacher from the class I mentioned at the art center."

Burke lifted the edge of the mattress and peeked beneath. No sign of a hex bag. "Where were his clothes?"

"He had the top two drawers there."

Both drawers remained full of neatly folded clothing. Neither held anything out of the ordinary.

Wanda's gaze darted to an overflowing laundry hamper in the corner. "What could be in his clothing that would hurt him?"

Burke held up her one good hand in a helpless gesture. "I'm sorry. I really don't know. We're just looking at all the details."

"I don't think we need to bother Mrs. Smithfield any further today." Gordon produced a business card from the inside pocket of his blazer and passed it to Wanda. "If you think of anything we should know, please don't hesitate to give us a call."

Burke could feel the energy coming off him. He'd seen something and wanted to tell her, but he didn't want to say it in front of the boy's mother. She thanked Wanda for her time, expressed her condolences, and kept a normal pace on her way back out to the car.

"What is it?" she asked the second he closed his door.

"The woman in that picture is Loretta."

"Loretta who?"

Gordon turned the key and cranked up the heat. "Loretta. You know, Stanley's Loretta. Don't you find it strange that the woman desperate to find a hunter was the teacher of the kid who was killed?"

Burke pulled the files from under the seat and peeked inside. "Well, let's see if we can find any sign of Loretta in the next house."

THE NEXT DOOR GORDON AND BURKE KNOCKED ON WAS that of Wade and Kaidence Campbell. If looks could kill, the glare Wade focused on them would have sent them to an early grave. While they introduced themselves, he stood with his fists balled at his sides.

When they were done speaking, he forced his words out through gritted teeth.

"My little girl spent the last two weeks of her life poked and prodded by every doctor in the state of Washington. Not one of them could do a damn thing to help. I'm done with doctors and—"

"With all due respect, Mr. Campbell, we're not doctors. We're investigators," Burke cut him off.

He tried to slam the door shut, but she jammed her foot in the doorway.

"Mr. Campbell, I am truly sorry for your loss. I can't imagine the pain you must be feeling, and I hate to intrude on you at this time, but we need to figure out what's happening, or more parents are going to suffer the same loss."

A muscle in his jaw jumped.

"Five minutes," Gordon said.

"Not a minute more, and so help me God, if you get my wife upset...." He let his unfinished threat hang in the space between them like a drop of poison suspended from the tip of a needle.

"We'll be as gentle as possible," Burke promised, and, at last, the man stepped back and let them enter the house.

He led them to a room shrouded in darkness. Heavy curtains shut out the faint daylight. A single low-wattage bulb in a table lamp next to a threadbare sofa provided the only illumination. Kaidence Campbell was curled into a ball next to the light. A photo album, thick with plastic pages, lay open on her lap. She never even looked up to see who had entered her house. Wade sat beside her on the sofa, leaving Burke and Gordon to stand. There were no other chairs in the small room.

Unlike the previous house, where signs of children littered every surface, if Burke hadn't known better, she would have assumed she was in the home of retirees. Nothing suggested a child had ever occupied this space. Within forty-eight hours of her death, every trace of the little girl had been wiped away.

Burke tried her best not to sound like someone *pretending* to be an official investigator. "As you said, Mr. Campbell, none of the doctors who attended your daughter, Amelia, could explain the cause of her illness, nor did the medical examiner find anything that he could explain. That's why we're here. Amelia's body gave us no clues about why the children in this area are getting sick. We don't know if it's a contagion, or an environmental factor, or something else entirely." All true statements, as far as that went. She shifted her weight to her other foot and told herself not to fidget. "We're trying to find any link at all between the children. It could be anything. Did they swim in the same pool? Attend the same church? Use the same kind of fingerpaint? Anything."

At last, Kaidence Campbell looked up at Burke. Her eyes were red and swollen as if she was suffering a bad case of conjunctivitis. "Amelia didn't fingerpaint. She was gifted and passed beyond that kind of stuff before she even started school." She shifted the book on her lap so that if Burke hunched awkwardly over the end table, she could see the glossy prints. "I know everybody keeps all their pictures on their phones these days, but when I was a kid, I just loved going through my mom's old photo albums. I thought it would be nice to have my own albums."

"There's a lot to be said for pictures you can hold in your hands," Burke said.

As Kaidence flipped through the pages, Burke tried to take in as many details as possible. Nearly every picture featured a tiny sprite of a child with long dark hair and solemn eyes. Here she was, riding a bicycle with training wheels. In oversized denim coveralls, grease all over her face, helping her father with some mechanical project. In a red and green Christmas dress, hair curled and held in place with an enormous velvet bow.

Kaidence stopped on a two-page spread of photos that showed her daughter holding up various works of art, drawings, clay pots, and paintings on canvas. For a child of eight, the work was exceptional in detail and creativity.

The idea of such brilliance, gone so early, caused physical pain in Burke's heart. "She had an amazing talent."

"There's more." Turning the page, Kaidence revealed a familiar face in one of the pictures.

"Who is that?" Burke asked, pointing.

"That's Ms. Youngblood."

"Loretta Youngblood?" Burke asked. "Doesn't she work at the children's art center in Forks?"

"I'm not sure. Maybe, but this was taken at Amelia's school. Ms. Youngblood taught an after-hours art program there. The two of them got along famously, two peas in a pod."

Burke stood upright and attempted to subtly stretch the kink out of her back. "One more question, and we'll leave you alone. Did anything strange happen in the days before Amelia took ill? Anything at all? Did she have nightmares or complain about being cold in a place that would normally be warm? Maybe she spoke about a bad smell or hearing something out of the ordinary?"

Kaidence had retreated into the world of pictures and memory. As far as Burke could tell, the grieving mother didn't even hear the question.

"Nothing, and five minutes is up." Wade stood and escorted them to the door. When they'd stepped outside, he slammed it hard enough to make the windows rattle.

"Friendly guy," Gordon said.

"I can't blame him. I have no idea what shape I'd be in if I were in his shoes."

"Fair enough." He extended a hand to help her down the porch steps.

Burke didn't need assistance, but she held his hand anyway. "Looks like we found our link."

"And it seems like it's part of a chain that leads back to Stanley."

Settling into the Cadillac's passenger seat, Burke couldn't help but roll her eyes. "You'd be surprised how often that happens."

"No," said Gordon in a somber tone that caught Burke by surprise. "I really wouldn't."

CHAPTER TWENTY-SEVEN

Richard

THE SQUEAK OF THE CABIN'S DOOR CAUGHT RICHARD OFF guard. He hadn't heard the car, but then again, Gordon had probably parked by the office due to the gigantic tree in the driveway. He popped out of the bathroom, curious to know if Burke and Gordon had learned anything of interest and found them standing inside the door with their mouths hanging open like they'd entered a fly-catching contest.

He tried to see through her eyes. In addition to the downed tree, a lamp lay shattered on the floor. Every surface in the cabin had been buried under a thick layer of dust. The salt circle had melted into a smelly crystallized mess. His reflection in the bathroom mirror revealed he was as messy as everything else—unruly hair sticking up every which way, his whole body brown with dirt, and a small oozing cut under his right eye.

Her head swiveled in Stanley's direction, and Richard's attention followed. He had to admit, seeing Stanley looking like a hot mess for once would be some good entertainment.

Richard frowned, disappointed. Stanley stood at the kitchen

sink, filling a bucket with soapy water. His bald head gleamed under the overhead lights. The crease in his khaki pants remained sharp as a knife edge. Even his fingernails were clean.

"You ripped your shirt," Burke said.

Examining the two-inch tear in his left sleeve, Stanley chuckled. "I never liked this shirt very much anyway."

"He's unnatural," Richard muttered. No one paid attention.

Gordon helped Burke out of her coat and hung it on the hook by the door.

"You guys going to tell us what happened?" She looked for a seat, but no surface remained clean.

"Allow me." Stanley carried the bucket to the kitchen table, dunked a rag in the soapy water, and washed the wooden chairs. "We used earth magic to try to get the totem to reveal its secrets. The object's magical properties magnified our spell, and the earth responded with gusto."

Gordon stood like a soldier at rest. "You're telling us you're the one who knocked that tree over outside."

"I was surprised by the magnitude of the amplification," Stanley said.

Richard harrumphed at the understatement and went back into the bathroom to clean himself up and put on a set of clothes that didn't feel like he'd spent the first half of the day rolling wet in the sand. By the time he returned in fresh sweatpants and a tee-shirt that smelled of the lavender detergent Burke favored, the table, all four chairs, and the kitchen counter were gleaming. Burke had taken a seat while Gordon swept the floor and Stanley wiped down the shelves of a small bookcase.

Thirsty and unsettled, Richard poured himself a glass of prune juice. He'd help with the cleaning but needed a minute more to work himself up to it.

Burke, in the middle of telling what they'd learned, continued. "So, Loretta is the only connection we see. She had clear ties to at least two of the children, and we know she has ties to you."

"I certainly had nothing to do with those children taking ill." Stanley squatted down to wipe the bottom shelf. Neither one of his knees popped.

Sitting next to Burke, Richard's bones made noises like a milk-filled bowl of Rice Krispies—as was proper for a body that had seen more than eighty years of life.

"We know you didn't do anything to harm the kids," Burke said. "But our first guess about who was behind all this was Busar, and you're definitely linked to Busar."

Stanley rose to his full height like a dancer and, taking hold of one of the drapes, shook it to dislodge the dust that had settled there.

Richard might have pointed out that he had just dirtied up the floor where Gordon had finished sweeping, but Stanley continued before he got the chance. "It's true that I'm linked to Busar, but we know for sure that Busar is not the one causing these troubles. He's locked safely away."

Richard drained his glass and wiped his mouth with the back of his hand. "You need to stop pussyfooting around and do what needs to be done."

They all stared at him like a lobster had just crawled out of his ear.

"Well, it's as clear as the nose on your face, ain't it?" he demanded.

No one answered.

He rolled his eyes. "You need to talk to Loretta. Whatever's going on, we ain't going to figure it out until you ask her what she knows. There's at least two more kids sick right this minute. There ain't no more time for putting it off because you ain't got the gumption to face your old girlfriend."

Stanley nodded in agreement. "I suppose you're right, Dick. I do need to speak with her, but I'm telling you all right now that there is no way that Loretta could be responsible for what's happening.

"She's an angel, an observer, sworn to watch humanity and to serve Heaven's command. She would never cause harm. I'm not even sure she could if she wanted to. It simply isn't in her nature."

How could a man fall for a woman incapable of doing bad things and for a woman who was evil incarnate. If whatever magic had touched Stanley rubbed off on Richard and gave him another hundred years on Earth, he still wouldn't understand.

"No one is accusing Loretta of anything." Burke shifted as if her bum arm was aching again. "But she's the only lead we have. Avoiding her is wasting time. What could it hurt to ask her what she knows? She's been here all along. Maybe she's got insights that we don't."

"No need to twist my arm, dear. I agree with you," Stanley replied. "I will insist on going alone, though. Some conversations aren't meant to be held in front of an audience."

Richard's mouth started moving before his brain could consider what he was saying. "You're just about two cards short of a barrel if you think I'm letting you run off on your own when there's umpteen monsters crawling the streets around here, and some witch is playing with us for their own entertainment, and a demigod with a sick sense of humor has it out for you."

"I never said Raven has a grudge against me." Stanley's eyes twinkled in that annoying way that always made Richard feel like he was being laughed at.

"Raven?" Gordon stopped sweeping and looked back and forth between them. "Who's Raven?"

Did they not cover that ground? Who could keep track of all these danged monsters anyway?

"If I didn't know better, I'd say you cared about my welfare," Stanley teased Richard, ignoring Gordon entirely.

"If you don't know that by now, you must be dumb as a stump," Richard growled. "Now, are you going to go talk to her, or are we going to hang out here declaring our undying love and devotion?"

Stanley lifted a pillow from the sofa and beat the dust out of it. "I do appreciate your concern, Dick, truly, but I really don't think—"

"Look, you done left Burke and me standing on the side of the road because you had some half-cocked plan to let The Devil kidnap you. You got yourself ripped in half trying to distract a bunch of demons when we had to get Burke out of that cage back in Michigan. You got blasted to the Canadian border and sent Gordon and me wandering around in the woods trying to find you. Enough of your stupid self-sacrifice and cockamamie plans. If you want me to sit in the car and wait, then that's what I'll do, but I'll be a suck-egg mule before I let you run off alone right now, leaving the rest of us behind to figure out what the heck is going on."

To Richard's ultimate horror, Stanley appeared to be on the verge of tears for a split second. Thankfully, the old fart pulled himself together and gave a little nod. "All right, then. I see there's no dissuading you." He replaced the pillow and clapped his hands together to rid them of grime. "Burke, Gordon, give us two hours, not one minute more. Do not add time for mishaps or bad communication. If we're not back in this cabin in exactly one hundred and twenty minutes, it's because we're in trouble."

Ever the literalist, Burke took her phone from her pocket and set the timer. "Clock's ticking."

CHAPTER TWENTY-EIGHT

Ben

THE OLD, BALD HUNTER PARKED HIS CAR AT THE CURB outside the house. The other gray-hair was with him, but no sign of the girl and the younger man. Why were there so many of them driving around together anyway? Not that it mattered. One hunter or a thousand wouldn't be able to stop the ball once it was rolling.

Eager to see his mother's reaction, Ben tiptoed out of his room and crept down the stairs to the landing. From there, without exposing himself, he could see the front door and a large area of the living room where his mother sat working on her latest crochet project and listening to a podcast about using herbs and other natural methods of healing.

Willow bark for a fever? What a fool she was. He could show her how to drop the temperature by forty degrees using willow along with a few other harder-to-come-by ingredients. She didn't believe in his power. She was afraid of it. She was ignorant, but she'd see. They would all see what he was capable of soon enough.

Where was the hunter, anyway? What was taking so long?

He'd turned halfway around to go back upstairs and looked out the window again to confirm that the big red boat was still out when the doorbell rang.

His mother set her project aside and used a voice command to silence the podcast. Too bad her back was to him when she opened the door. He saw her surprise in the stiffening of her posture and the subtle half-step back but seeing it on her face would have been much better.

Baldy stood alone on the front step. Apparently, his buddy decided to wait in the car. Interesting.

"Hello, Loretta." He spoke in a low baritone, heavy with the pronunciation of British royalty.

Mother lifted a hand to her mouth and then dropped it again. "I prayed you would come."

"It turns out that, at this advanced age, life is teaching me to stop running away," Baldy said.

"You didn't have to run from me." She spoke so quietly Ben could barely hear her. Sap and drama. Disgusting. These two had what was coming to them.

"It wasn't you I was running from." He slipped his hands into the pockets of his fancy, fitted coat with the upturned collar. "May I come in?"

"Oh!" Mother acted as if she'd forgotten she was in her own house. She lost her ability to reason the moment this deadbeat showed his face. She'd been dreaming of this moment for decades, like some lovesick teenager with a crush on a rockstar. *Someday he'll come back. He's a great man. You'll see.*

Ben didn't see greatness. He saw an arrogant coward. The marvelous Stanley Kapcheck was about to learn some tough and long-overdue lessons.

She held the door open while he passed. She took his coat from him and hung it on the rack with her jackets and scarves.

They settled onto opposite ends of the sofa with their bony old-people knees pointed toward the middle.

"How have you been?" Stanley asked.

"Fine. Not much has changed."

"You're as lovely as you ever were."

A deep blush rose to her cheeks. "And you're the same smooth liar I met a long time ago."

"No, Loretta. I've never lied to you. I never could."

Silence stalked into the room, a big, hulking presence. It plopped down between them, making a mockery of their long pauses, rich with meaning, and their adolescent fidgeting.

At last, Mother broached a subject worthy of conversation. "Are you here because of the children?"

"Yes." He rubbed a hand over his head. "Well, sort of. I've been watching the area. I saw reports of the first death and hoped it was natural. Around that time, I bumped into Christine."

Mother gasped. "Just by coincidence?"

"You and I both know that only fools believe in coincidence." He sighed and settled back into the corner of the couch, making himself comfortable in Ben's home. "I have, from time to time over the years, been arrogant enough to ignore signs when they were sent to me. It never ends well. This sign was"—he waved one hand in the air like he was wielding a net that might have the power to catch the words he needed—"it was flashing neon. What could I do? I'm done with running, Loretta."

"I'm glad to hear that." She twisted the fabric of her peasant skirt around her fingers like a nervous schoolgirl.

"Please tell me about Busar," he said.

"What do you want to know? I haven't seen him in years."

The wrinkled Lothario inched closer to Ben's mother. "My friends told me what you said in the restaurant, but you must know something, anything."

"I wish I did. What I told them was pretty much everything." Glancing down coyly, she tucked a loose lock of hair behind her ear. "At least, I think I did. It's all kind of a blur. Stanley, I saw your car, and I think I came unhinged. I barely remember barging into that restaurant. I was in shock."

Leaving her comments unmentioned, the hunter chewed the subject of his messed-up friend like a dog chews its favorite bone. "What was he like when you saw him?"

She shrugged. "Like you'd expect. He was broken. The energy around him carried a weight like the air before a thunderstorm, but he tried so hard. He said all the right things. Every step was placed with careful deliberation."

"But that wasn't enough, was it?"

"I really don't know."

The silence between them was different now, no longer dark and frightening but filled with the tension of lovers who'd left things unresolved. It set Ben's teeth on edge and made him want to scream, stab, and burn. He bit his lip hard between his teeth and shifted to a more comfortable position. He could have set off a bomb without the two reunited lovebirds noticing. They wouldn't pay any attention to a kid sitting on the stairs.

"Why did he lock himself up?" Stanley asked.

Ben's mother put a hand to her heart. "Is that what he did? I had no idea. He was around, and then he wasn't. I couldn't even tell you how long it took me to realize that. One day it just occurred to me that I hadn't seen him in a long time." She pressed the wrinkled fabric of her skirt smooth again. "Busar wasn't the man who occupied my thoughts."

The hunter had the audacity to reach out and take her hand. "I shouldn't have left you like I did, Loretta. I'm sorry. I was—"

"I was pregnant."

Ben's vision blacked for a moment, then it narrowed as if he was looking through a telescope focused on Stanley Kapcheck's face. Never in a million years would he have guessed his mother would just blurt it. All the blood drained from Stanley's already pale cheeks. The corners of his mouth twitched, as if he were trying to decide if his ex-girlfriend was playing some sick joke on him.

"We have a son, Stanley."

Stanley shook his head. His smile turned sad, a look of pity. "Oh, my dear. I'm sorry, but that can't be true."

She drew back from him, pulling her hand out of his grasp. Ben hoped she'd smack him, but she remained sickeningly gentle. "Of course, it's true."

"It can't be. I was terribly ill with the mumps as a young man. More than once, I've been told by medical professionals that I can't father a child."

Ben scooted down one step to hear better. Surely his mother hadn't made such a colossal mistake.

His mother cocked her head and raised a brow at Stanley. "And you, with your life experience, believe that human medical professionals understand all there is to know about this world and how it works?" She shook her head. "I'm an angel, Stanley. It's not your body that…I mean…. For my kind, it is the connection of the heart that gives way to new life; the purity of love, too great to be contained, gives rise to a new being."

Maybe the old man would have a stroke and die right there on the living room floor. That would be sort of funny, but ultimately, that would ruin everything Ben had worked all these years to achieve. Hopefully, the geezer could hold himself together.

"I know that Ben is your son, Stanley. There's no mistake, but I'm worried."

The hunter frowned. "He must be a grown man, thirty years old now."

"Something's wrong with him." Her voice cracked, and a single tear spilled from her eye.

Ben's guts twisted. He scooted forward another step and wrapped his arms around his aching midsection.

"Is he ill?" Stanley looked like he'd taken a series of hard hits to the head as if struggling to figure out which way was up.

Mother stifled a sob. "He was the sweetest, smartest little boy I'd ever seen, Stanley. He had all of humanity's bravery and curiosity, and all of Heaven's love and wonder. But lately...something.... He's not possessed. I would know, but some kind of evil has taken root in him. It's festered"—she sniffed and wiped her wet cheeks—

"he's evil, Stanley. He's a bad man and powerful, and I'm afraid of him."

The pain in Ben's core shattered, jagged shards piercing him, forcing a wretched scream from his lips, driving him into the small room where his mother and father sat leaning toward one another, imparting their most closely held secrets. "Is that what you think of me?" He tossed the coffee table aside and stood before them, trembling, weeping, teeth grinding together. "You think I'm evil? A thing to be feared?"

Ignoring the man, he focused on the woman who'd betrayed him. "Would you have this hunter destroy me? He can try. He won't succeed. He's nothing. A pitiful mortal with an unusual streak of luck that's kept him alive this long. All my life I've watched you mourn this rube. You've spun stories about how fabulous he was. And now he's here, and I see for myself that he's no more than a sad excuse for a human with one foot already in the grave."

To vent some of the energy pulsing through him, he snatched the crystal candy dish off the end table and sent it flying into the wall where it burst into a thousand glittering bits of worthless glass. Worthless, just like Stanley Kapcheck.

"I found a way to bring him back to you," he shouted. "It was me who figured out how to give you the one thing you truly wanted. I sacrificed more than—" No. He wouldn't reveal that.

Some secrets were meant to be kept until the grave, and even beyond. "It's because of me that your precious Stanley is here with you, and you call me evil? How dare you?"

He sensed Stanley's subtle shift. Before the hunter could make his move, Ben grabbed his mother by the throat and, with his free hand pointed at his father. "I swear to you, if you move another inch, I will send her back to her maker in Heaven."

"When you say you made this happen, what do you mean?" Stanley asked. "Are you the one responsible for the sick children?"

Of course, the hunter was short-sighted. Of course, he fixated on the kids. "I did what I had to do. I didn't want those kids to get hurt, but sometimes, in a war, there's collateral damage. That's a risk every strategist has to assume."

"If it's not about the kids, tell me what it's about," Stanley demanded.

Pride swelled in Ben's heart. He couldn't stay mad, or hold his mother in a death grip, not in the face of the joy his plan brought him. He flung her onto the sofa. "I figured out a way to fix it. I can fix all of it, every bad thing that ever happened. The price was high to get this far, and it will be higher still before it's all over, but it will be worth it."

"What did you do, Ben?" Mother ran a hand over her throat. He'd been hasty to threaten her. He must not let his emotions get the better of him, or he may ruin his plan.

"I fixed your problem, Mother. I brought you your heart's desire. And, in doing so, I fixed a far bigger problem, as well." That wasn't entirely true. No point in lying. "Well, I haven't fixed it yet, but I will. Everything is in place now."

"Oh, do tell," Stanley urged. "I love a happy ending."

"Happy endings are great, but every good story has some tragedy along the way," Ben retorted.

"Like a few dead children?"

Ben balled his hands into fists and willed himself to stay in control. "I told you, I had no choice. Do you have to keep coming back to that? It's not about the kids, you damn fool old man. If you weren't such an idiot, this would be over already."

Stanley crossed his legs and folded his hands over his stomach. "Educate me."

Pacing in front of the couch, trying to burn off some small portion of the energy that burned like molten lava in his veins, he explained only the parts they needed to know. "I learned from my mother that you came here to fight a monster that couldn't be fought. You had a powerful magical item, and in your arrogance, you thought that you could wield it, but the magic destroyed your friend. It ripped him apart and left him trapped between worlds. I thought about that for a long time. If the object left half of him here, where did the other half go?" He smirked at Stanley. "Did *you* ever figure it out?"

"The other half is inside the totem," Stanley said.

"Well done. How long did that take you?"

"Too long."

Ben went on, perched on the edge of a chair, heels bouncing with pent-up energy. "If I could control that totem, I could control the creature it made. But I didn't know the spell you used. I needed you so I could learn how the trap was created. I couldn't just play around guessing at it, or I might end up no better than the animal in the cave out in the woods, right?

"For a while, I worried about that. Once I learned the spell, then what? But then it came to me. My own dear mother has the strength to work that kind of magic. I thought, maybe, if I sent you to him, showed you that he was alive, you'd do the rest on your own, but I realize now what a long shot that was. Clearly, you don't have the vision to understand what Busar could accomplish."

His mother rose from the couch with the slow, deliberate movements of a sleepwalker. "You murdered those innocent babies to lure Stanley here? You expect him to help you turn his best friend into a slave? And you think I'll help?" She took a single step closer. "To what purpose, Ben? What do you want to accomplish in the end?"

He stood to face her, eye-to-eye. "I did this for you, Mother. I brought Stanley to you. The least you could do is say thank you."

"Thank you?" Sweat broke out across her upper lip. "Why did you do this, really? Not to bring Stanley back to us. Tell me why."

"I did it for you."

"Stop lying and tell me what you hoped to achieve!" Blue waves of electricity danced along her arms, flaring from her fingertips in flashes that forced him to squint and turn away.

CHAPTER TWENTY-NINE

Richard

SOME FOLKS MIGHT THINK WAITING IN THE CAR WOULD BE torture. There was a time when Richard might have agreed with them, but truth be told, he'd come to enjoy it. The hunter's life meant a lot of time in tiny spaces with Stanley, Burke, and now Gordon, too. Having his folks around him was fine, but after living on his own for the past half-century, he'd gotten used to the sound of his own silence. Plus, the car was cool. The seats were comfortable, the radio was superb, and the vehicle was just about as big as his room at the old folks' home had been, so he never felt cramped hanging out in there by himself.

The most difficult part was staying focused on what he was supposed to be watching. Sometimes he got so comfortable he drifted off for a few minutes. He was doing pretty good today, though, keeping his eyes on Loretta's little two-story house with the white picket fence while listening to Paul Harvey tell The Rest of The Story. Thank God for radio stations that replayed the good stuff.

Paul got to the part about General Santa Ana popping a bit of chicle into his mouth because chewing quieted his nerves when a flash of blue light flickered in Loretta's living room window.

"Could be the television," he muttered, but what kind of sense would that make? Stanley shows up at his lover's doorstep three decades after turning tail, and they settle in to watch the afternoon soaps? Not likely.

A more probable scenario was that Stanley was in trouble. After all, Stan Kapcheck spent a great deal more time getting himself into trouble than he did watching television.

Richard switched off the radio and pulled the keys from the ignition. He opened the trunk, lifted the false bottom, and looked over their weapons stash. What the heck would he be fighting? The angel? If that was the case, nothing in this pile of wood and metal would do him any good.

Busar? Nah. The way Stanley and Burke described it, the old hunter was locked up tighter than a nun's knees. If it was the boogeyman, Richard stood even less chance than if they had to fight the angel.

Might be the witch that left the hex bag on the porch. Figuring he may as well go with that theory since it was the only scenario that offered him a slim chance of survival, he lifted a Smith and Wesson long barrel .38 special loaded with bullets etched with symbols that would let them pass through magical warding.

Richard hurried, hoping none of the neighbors paid too much attention to the old man with the very big gun creeping up to the single lady's house. A quick peek in the tall, slim window next to the front door gave him a glimpse of a young man standing nose-to-nose with Loretta, who looked like she got caught inside a ball of lightning. So far as Richard could tell, Stanley appeared to be reclining on the sofa, taking in the show.

If he opened the door, the movement would catch someone's attention. He didn't have much going for him, so holding on to the element of surprise seemed pretty important.

Back down the concrete steps and around the corner of the house, past a row of rose bushes trimmed down to nubs, he found the back door, and praise be, it was unlocked. Careful to be as quiet as he could, he inched the door open and stepped into Loretta's tidy kitchen that smelled of coffee and cinnamon.

The damp rubber soles of his shoes threatened to squeak on the ceramic tiles, giving him away, so keeping hold of his gun with his right hand and clinging to the kitchen counter with his left hand for balance, he toed them off and left them on the mat before proceeding to the archway that led to the combined dining/living room.

"Why can't you understand? You're my mother. You're an angel. Why is it so hard? You, of all people, should be able to see the big picture." The young guy was whining and making sad puppy eyes at Loretta.

Stanley stood and slipped his hands into the pockets of his slacks. "Ben, what you've done, no ends can justify that."

"Stay out of this," the young guy yelled like a petulant teenager, though he appeared to be a good ten years past adolescence. "This part of it doesn't have anything to do with you."

"I thought it all had to do with me, with me and my relationship with your mother. Me and my relationship with Busar. No matter which way you look at it, it's about me, and perhaps, it's about your feelings about me?"

"I did it for my mother!"

"Maybe that's how it started, but the magic you used was of a dark and unstable nature. Listen to yourself. Your logic, the reasons you spout, don't even make sense. There's a reason for that, Ben."

"You don't know."

"I do know. I've dealt with dark magic, too. At first, it seems like a power you can manage, but gone too far, you become a slave. The magic changes you, controls you, urges you on to ever more grandiose acts, each more horrific than the one before. So, what's your end game, Ben? What does the magic want you to do?"

The kid's body shook like he was slipping into an epileptic fit.

Richard shifted to get a better angle if he needed to take a shot, and his toe hit the doorframe. He sucked in a sharp breath, and then all eyes were on him.

Blue eyes narrowed in pure hatred and met Richard's gaze. "You're one element that isn't needed for my spell." He reached one hand out toward Richard, palm up. "*Mors, venit ad—*"

Richard didn't have the foggiest idea what that meant, but he'd have bet his bippy it was nothing good. He aimed the revolver and cocked the hammer.

"No!" Stanley planted one foot on the seat of the sofa and vaulted right over the back, but Richard's finger had already squeezed around the trigger, and the extraordinary bang echoed off the walls of Loretta's living room.

CHAPTER THIRTY

Burke

BURKE PUT HER RIGHT FOOT ON THE CHAIR IN THEIR ROOM and let Gordon strap her around her ankle. "I can't believe it never occurred to us to figure out exactly how we would follow them if they didn't come back in time. We're off our game." She tugged her pant leg down over the weapon and stepped back. "Now's just about the worst time for us to be distracted."

"Am I a distraction?"

She raised a brow. "Of course you are. You are. This stupid arm is. Stanley's jacked-up history with half the supernatural females on Earth is a distraction. We're a mess."

He grasped her shoulders and kissed her forehead. "I've got an idea about the car. Let me prove I'm an asset, not just a distraction."

His words sent a pang of guilt straight into her heart. "I didn't mean it like that."

"I know. It's okay. I'll be right back."

"No." She grabbed his arm. "We stay together. No more splitting up. Nothing good ever comes of it."

"You know, they still have fifteen minutes. Maybe everything is fine."

"Do you believe that?" she asked, half hoping he'd lie and tell her that's exactly what he believed.

"Not really, no."

Dammit.

They left the cabin hand-in-hand and made their way around the fallen tree across the driveway and over to the office/store.

The diminutive man with the epic beard looked up from the Finn O'Doyle paperback he held in his left hand. "Howdy. What can I do for you?"

"We need a car," Gordon said.

"Well, up in Forks, there's—"

"No." Gordon shook his head. "We need a car right now. It's an emergency, but we'll have it back to you later tonight."

The man's gaze darted between Gordon and Burke as if he was trying to decide whether or not they were pulling a prank on him. "This isn't an Enterprise lot."

"I thought maybe you could loan us your car," Gordon said.

"Well, I don't know about that." The man wrapped the end of his beard around the fingers of his right hand.

Burke took five hundred-dollar bills from her wallet and laid them on the counter.

The man laughed. "Shoot. I'll sell you the old rustbucket for that much."

"We'll have it back to you tonight," Gordon said.

With a shrug, the guy dug his keys out of his pocket, removed the largest from the keyring, and laid it on the counter. "She stalls if you idle too long. Gotta keep one foot on the gas."

Burke thanked him on her way out the door.

"They've still got four minutes," Gordon said.

"Screw that. Let's go." She yanked open the passenger's door of the two-tone rust and blue Toyota pickup that was the only vehicle in the lot and climbed in, but before Gordon could follow, the Cadillac turned into the lot, and Stanley parked next to the truck. Burke was back out in a flash. "Cut it kind of close, didn't you?

"Apologies," Stanley said. He'd already gotten out of the driver's seat and stood with his arms on the vehicle's cloth top. "Things were a bit more complicated than we anticipated."

"Aren't they always?"

Richard's door creaked open. He planted one hand on the door and one on the car's frame and hauled himself out with a grunt. An attractive older woman, that had to be Loretta, emerged from the back. A single shadowy figure remained slumped in the back seat.

"Who've you got there?" Burke demanded.

Richard peeked inside the car like he wasn't entirely sure who she was talking about before dropping a bomb on her. "That's Stan's kid. He's a witch. Tried to kill me, but we've got him tranqued and tied up with warded cuffs now."

Words failed. Burke stared at Stanley with her mouth hanging open like an idiot. He dropped his face into his hand and rubbed his eyes. Loretta shifted her weight and stared at her toes.

Gordon cleared his throat. "How about we go inside the cabin and get this sorted out." He jogged back into the office, presumably to return the proprietor's car keys.

By the time he returned, Stanley and Richard had the young man out of the car, propped between them like a drunk getting walked out of a bar at closing time. They dragged him along the driveway, up the cabin stairs, through the door, and dropped him unceremoniously on the couch. His eyes rolled up in his head, and drool formed along the right corner of his mouth.

No one spoke as they shed coats and found places to sit in a haphazard circle of upholstered furniture and kitchen chairs.

Burke sank into one of the soft chairs, biting her lip to stifle a groan. She'd lost track of what painkillers she'd taken when, but somewhere along the line, she'd concluded that Stanley had done a bad job of it, and the break in her shoulder was not healing like it should. Heaven only knew what kind of mess she'd be once she could get rid of the stupid sling.

Loretta, perched on one of the wooden chairs with her ankles crossed like a princess, leaned toward her. "May I?"

"Loretta, you can't," Stanley shot to his feet like she'd just drawn a double-edged sword.

The smile she offered him held an immensity of pain and grief, so intense empathetic tears burned in Burke's eyes, although she had no idea what was going on.

"But I can, Stanley. I can do so many things, and up until now, I've sat around and watched."

"Your job is to sit around and watch. If you use your—"

"Stanley Kapcheck, I don't need you to remind me of the consequences of my actions; thank you."

Stan dropped into his chair as if she'd slapped him across the face.

"I know what will happen," she said. "I will deal with that after I help you deal with this. I will not continue to let horrible things happen when I have the ability to stop them."

Before Burke realized what the woman intended, or before she answered whether Loretta had permission to work her magic, the angel had her hands pressed to Burke's damaged shoulder.

A flash of pain so exquisite it spoke of death as a sweet release from the horror of life shot through Burke like a lightning bolt, followed by a warm light of such pure intensity everything outside of it ceased to exist. Burke could neither hear nor see. The chair beneath her disappeared. The men in the room vanished. The room vanished. It had never existed at all. The only thing that remained, the only thing that had ever been, the only thing that would ever be, was a love wider than the universe and higher than the heavens. Love washed away the Big Bang and took with it every moment of violent birth and death that followed. Everything she ever thought she knew was an illusion, less real than images made of dust, for at least dust had form.

Loretta stepped away, and Burke remembered to draw breath, which she did in a great shuddering gasp. Her body—real flesh in the physical world—demanded that of her. The men stared at her. Three men. Men who embodied the love she'd nearly drowned in. Concern was written across their faces.

"Is it better now?" Loretta asked.

Burke looked to the lovely, elderly woman who'd arrived with Stanley and Richard. Gone were the signs of age and earthly wear and tear. She stood there, ageless, perfect, glowing softly with gentle blue light.

"Your shoulder should be fine now."

Stanley turned away abruptly and went to stand near one of the windows, gazing out toward the relentless gray sea.

Flexing her arm slowly and with great care at first, and then in larger motions, Burke realized that her shoulder was pain-free, and her body hummed with strength. If a coven of vampires burst through the door at that moment, she was confident she could deal with them single-handedly and unarmed. But that would mean killing something within the same great love she'd witnessed. She was part of that love, not just a receiver of it, but that love was her, and she was it, and so were they. The tears that threatened spilled over now, rivers that ran down her cheeks unchecked.

"It's okay. The feeling will fade to a manageable level," Loretta promised.

At that, Burke cried even harder. She tried to excuse herself and ended up mumbling unintelligibly. Finally, she escaped to her bedroom to catch her breath.

The room was cool, and the drapes were pulled shut, making it dark as twilight. Burke sat on the edge of the bed and cried, wiping her face with tissues from the pink and gray box on the nightstand. Sobs turned to sniffles, and after a minute more, the sniffles dried up, leaving Burke not empty as she'd expect after a total meltdown but washed clean.

Blowing her nose one final time, she realized she was holding the tissue with both hands. She discarded the sling in the little black plastic trash can and returned to the main area of the cabin in time to hear her grandfather yell at the guy in handcuffs. He was awake now but still bound.

"You must be nuttier than a squirrel turd if you think we're going to put that thing in your hands."

Gordon jumped to his feet and met her near the bedroom door. He pressed his hands to her cheeks and looked into her eyes, as if trying to catch a glimpse of her soul. "Are you okay?"

With total honesty, Burke assured him that she'd never been better in her life.

The guy in the cuffs sounded amused. "You don't have any choice. I have all the answers, and you have exactly zero power to do anything about any of this."

"Sum up for me," Burke said in a low voice to Gordon.

Gordon answered in a whisper that could carry no further than Burke's ears. "The guy on the couch is our witch. He's Stanley and Loretta's love child. Apparently, she's been pining for Stan all these years, and the kid wanted to take matters into his own hands, but whatever magic he used broke him. Now he's got some sort of crackpot scheme that none of us can exactly figure out. He wants us to give him the totem and open Busar's cage, but he won't say why."

"Grandpa's right. We'd be insane to do that."

"Agreed, but Ben's the one killing the kids, and we don't know what kind of spell he's using to do it. That's about as far as we've gotten."

"Stop this!" Loretta's voice shook the cabin's walls, and all eyes turned to her. "What is your ultimate goal, Benjamin? Be truthful."

"I only wanted to bring you and Stanley together." His bottom lip trembled like a child's.

"Here we are, together, and yet you persist."

"Stanley is still distracted. He needs to free Busar. With the totem and the spell, I could—"

"I won't give you that power," Stanley spoke without turning from the window.

"We ought to just turn this nut job over to the cops," Richard suggested. "He's a killer, right?"

Burke strolled toward the group but didn't sit down. She had too much energy for sitting. "No court in the world could convict him. Witch trials aren't a thing anymore."

"Maybe they ought to be," Richard muttered.

The waves of love still crashed against the shore of Burke's heart. "We can't just kill him; he's human."

Ben twisted his body to get to a more upright position against the back of the couch. "I can save the two kids who are sick right now."

They all stared at him, waiting.

"They're probably recovering already. I sapped their energy with a spell, but I haven't cast it in two days. If I don't cast it again, it's likely both of them still have enough strength left that their bodies will heal and restore themselves."

Stanley turned, leaned against the window frame, and slipped his hands into his pockets. "But if we don't cooperate, at a word from you, they'll be gone."

"I didn't say that."

"You didn't have to."

Loretta covered her face with her hands.

Burke said, squaring her shoulders and lifting her chin, "I think we should do it."

Now everyone stared at her. Even Loretta peeked up at her.

"Busar is your friend, Stanley, your family. If there's a chance he can be healed, we need to take it." She turned to Loretta. "Can you use the totem without being hurt?"

"No power in Heaven or Earth can hurt me in this form."

Burke believed her. The waves of energy pulsed in the room, raising the hairs on her arms and the back of her neck.

She turned to the man who sat bound before them. "I don't know what your game is, witch. I'm not even sure you know what it is. You've played with power that ought not be played with, and it's left you addled. I pity you."

"I don't need your pity, hunter." Gone were the pleading eyes and pouty lips. He was all anger and wrath now.

Burke ignored his ire. "Maybe, in the beginning, you really did want to bring your parents together. Now, something is using you for some other purpose. Whatever that is, when it comes to light, we will stop it."

"I will be the beast, rising from the sea. I will usher in the end of the world with laughter." There was nothing sane or human left in his eyes.

She smiled at him. "You seem to be operating under the delusion that we don't know how to stop the end of the world." Leaning toward him, she dropped her voice to a whisper. "We've stopped the end of the world before. We'll do it again. That's our job."

When she stood straight again, Stanley met her eye.

"Are you ready to do this?" she asked.

He nodded. "It's time."

CHAPTER THIRTY-ONE

Richard

ONE OF THE GOOD THINGS ABOUT THE CADILLAC IS THAT there was never a shortage of space. Longer than the average pickup truck and wider than the average minivan, the car was roomy enough to sit three across each bench seat without feeling cramped.

Stanley drove with Burke beside him and Gordon to her right. Richard found himself stuck in the backseat with the angel and the witch. He fiddled with his hearing aid and pushed his false teeth inside his mouth for a while. The silence ate at him. No matter that the car was big. They could have been riding in a Prevost bus, and it still wouldn't have been large enough to contain the awkwardness.

He looked at Loretta, "I ain't never met an angel before. I knew when I first met you that you weren't an average lady, but I wouldn't have guessed your kind walk around down here."

Loretta pressed her hands together between her knees. "We are few. Most prefer to stay in Heaven. A few have fallen."

"Fallen, eh? So that really is how it all happened?"

She stared out the window, and Richard gave up. He didn't have anything to say to the witch.

The road wound northward, hugging the coasts, sometimes weaving inland a mile or two, but before it turned east and paralleled the Canadian border, Stanley took a right onto an unpaved service road. For another twenty minutes, they bumped along in the weird, dim greenish light. It occurred to Richard that, once again, they were entering the forest as the sun dipped westward. Probably not a sign of their vast intelligence that they kept doing the same stupid thing over and over.

At the end, the road just petered out to nothing.

"We walk from here," Stanley announced, and they all piled out of the car and trooped along behind him like scouts, following their leader deeper into the woods.

For a while, keeping up was no problem. Richard put one foot in front of the other, concentrating on not tripping and busting up his one good hip, but after a while, a tightness formed in his belly. He'd drank his prune juice that day, and it had done the trick, so he wasn't sure what the problem could be, but tightness grew to pain, and pain was fast shifting to fear. He was about to say something when the witch growled.

"I can't get through." He twitched as if bugs were crawling on him. "I knew this space was warded, but what is this? What the hell is out here?"

Stanley slipped his hands into his pockets. "This is dryad territory. They've protected it against dark magic."

Falling to his knees, teeth gritted against some unseen foe, Ben shook his head back and forth in short, tight snaps. "It's burning me."

Crystal teardrops slid down Loretta's ethereal cheeks like streaks of glitter. She held a handout to her son. "Take my hand, Ben."

When he didn't reach toward her, she bent and wrapped her fingers around his.

His shoulders relaxed, and he looked around as if startled.

"I will shield you as long as I can," she said softly.

"What happens when you can't?"

With her left hand, she brushed the tears away, but she didn't answer.

Ben stood and took a hesitant step and then another.

Richard used the lull in the action as a chance to catch up to Stanley. "I got a real bad feeling about this, Stan."

"That's wisdom speaking."

"Well, if my wisdom says we shouldn't be doing this, why are we doing it?"

"Sometimes fortune favors the bold," Stanley said.

"You're a dang fool, daft old man."

"You're most likely correct."

"Do you know how to get Busar out of that cage?"

Stanley shook his head. "No."

"Do you know how to put him back together again?"

"No."

"Do you know if it's true that that thing can't hurt Loretta?"

"No."

"Seems to me you know about as much as dog catcher in a rocket science lab," Richard muttered.

"Probably less." Stanley pointed toward a rocky hill. "It's just over there, in the little valley. Don't get too close to Busar. His condition is unstable."

Richard had never been one to curse excessively but venting his frustration with Stanley and his anxiety over the entire situation by muttering a few choice words felt appropriate to the moment.

They crested the hill like five overgrown hobbits hiking into Rivendell. They gazed down at the clutter of bones spread across the barren ground. To their left and below them, the cave with its heavy iron bars gaped like a mouth with teeth that grew from top jaw to bottom, stuck wide open in an eternal scream.

"He's stuck in there?" Loretta asked.

"Busar!" Stanley's shout died in the air as if the enormous trees had feasted on the sudden sound.

Dark hands wrapped around the bars. The rest of the man remained lost in shadow. "You were a fool to come back here, Stanley."

"I've been told that a lot lately."

"You will die here."

Stanley tugged his stocking cap down a little lower over his head. "Everybody's got to go sometime."

"How nice of you to bring an entourage. Is the angel here to usher your souls to Heaven?" He stepped closer to the bars, revealing the whites of his eyes and a flashy display of teeth. "I didn't expect you to go native, Loretta."

"I can help you," Loretta said.

"A miracle? For me? You're too kind, really, but if you were going to save me, you should have stepped in thirty years ago."

"I couldn't." She lifted her chin. "I was pregnant thirty years ago."

Busar's deep laughter reverberated through the wilderness. "Only you, Stanley Kapcheck. Only you." He reveled in his mirth a moment longer before going on. "What's been done to me cannot be undone. I am lost."

"We can use the totem. It's been restored," Stanley said.

In the silence, no bird sang. No cricket chirped.

"You're a fool, Stanley Kapcheck. That magic cannot be reversed," Busar said.

"We have the spell. We have the totem," Stanley argued.

"You'll be destroyed."

Loretta stepped toward the valley but stopped when Ben did not move with her. "I won't be destroyed. Not in this form."

"You'll face worse than destruction." Busar pressed against the bars now.

"My course is set. I will see you free before I go on my way."

"All of you need to go on your way, now. This is a bad idea. Leave me here."

Stanley opened the messenger bag slung across his shoulder and produced the box containing the totem. "I told you. I'm not leaving you again." With salt, he drew a devil's trap on the ground. "Ben, you can stand in the circle and be unaffected by the dryad magic."

"But I can't leave the circle?" Ben asked.

"I'm not going to leave you here, Benjamin." Loretta led him to the circle, and he stepped inside without further argument. She faced the cave. "I recommend you all back away."

Richard didn't need to be told twice. He high tailed it to the other end of the valley with Burke and Gordon at his heels.

"Think we ought to draw our guns?" he whispered.

"If this goes sideways, I don't think guns are going to help us," Burke replied.

Dang kid. Sometimes she was a real pessimist.

Loretta glided down the hillside like a movie star walking the red carpet and laying one hand on each of the two center bars, she popped them out of the stone as easily as picking toothpicks out of cheese squares.

"Where does Stanley find these women?" he wondered aloud.

Burke shrugged. "Hunters are led to their hunts."

Richard thought about the only woman his hunts ever led him into the arms of and shuddered. She'd tried to murder him, and darn near succeeded. Then again, the same could be said about Stanley and The Devil. Stan was just the kind of weirdo who seemed turned on by that level of crazy.

Busar edged out of the cave sideways and gazed around as if

to reassure himself the world was still whole and unchanged. "This is a bad idea," he said again.

Loretta ignored him. She opened the box on the ground by her feet and withdrew the totem. Blue light shimmered along her arms and encompassed the carved object. Before Stanley could say a thing, the totem sent out a high-pitched hum.

A sudden understanding of what was about to happen dawned on Richard. "Hit the dirt!"

Burke and Gordon dropped like trained marines responding to a call of "grenade!"

A column of light exploded out of the totem that lifted itself from Loretta's hands and hovered in the air. Dirt, leaves, and bits of bone flew into the sky, smacked against the canopy, and rained down on them.

When the ruckus finally calmed enough that Richard felt safe lifting his head, he peeked over at the trio standing by the cave entrance.

Busar's deep laugh rolled through the valley again. "I am unchanged, Stanley. I told you, you're a fool."

CHAPTER THIRTY-TWO

Ben

Unable to contain his glee, Ben bounced on his toes like a child on Christmas morning, beholding a splendor of gifts wrapped in glittering paper. He covered his mouth to hold in his joyous laughter, but it was impossible. After all this time, all the work and sacrifice, Busar was free!

"What have you done?"

His mother stood in front of him. Her fiery eyes—no longer human—studied him with an intensity that would have shaken a lesser man.

"I set him free. I gave you Stanley, and I gave Stanley Busar. Now everyone has what they want." A giggle bubbled from his lips, and he clamped down on it. "Including me."

"What have you done?" Blue lightning shot through the trees. Loretta's angelic voice bulldozed through the forest, sending flocks of birds scattering.

Ben wouldn't be intimidated. She might have some kind of Heavenly magic, but Ben held Earth in his hand, and that's where they stood. She was in his home court. "My goal, all along, was to find a way to free Busar. I figured Stanley would get him out of there, but it's even more fantastic that you did it." The days leading up to this glorious moment replayed in his mind. "I had a few worrisome moments, not the least of which was when the old man said he had a way to restore this beast to some kind of humanity but, just look"—he gestured at the *thing* standing outside its cage, naked and filthy, powerful, trembling with barely contained rage—"Busar will set the world on fire."

Like a naive child, the girl hunter cocked her head and frowned. "Why would you want that?"

Ben stepped toward her before remembering that he couldn't leave the salt circle. That was a problem, but he had no doubt he would figure it out, given enough time. "Why would you not want to destroy the world? The world is a disaster. Monsters and humans, gods, and devils, blah, blah, blah, all constantly fighting, jockeying for position, trying to scramble to a higher position in the food chain, and for what? They all die anyway. Nothing lasts."

He met his mother's fearsome gaze again. "Doesn't one of your boss's minions say as much in the Good Book? All of this is no more than chasing after the wind."

"But the fear of the Lord is the beginning of wisdom."

With a grin, he leaned toward her. "The Lord's not here, is he? Fear me. I'm a god now." Taking a page from his good old dad's book, he slipped his hands into his pockets to show the world how cool and nonchalant he could be in the face of a tough situation. "I've won, Mother. Busar is free. He lacks the willpower to put himself back in that cage, I guarantee it. And not even you, with all your buzzing blue energy, can kill him." He jerked his chin in the direction of the scattered bones. "Everywhere he goes, everything he does, every breath he takes will lead to the destruction of some living thing. It will build and grow exponentially, and he knows it. That's why he hid himself away in the first place. He thought he could manage it, and then one day, just driving past a logging field, he made a hundred and thirteen men die." Ben snapped his fingers. "Just like that."

The angel and the humans stared at him, speechless, too weak, too stupid, too lacking in vision to comprehend a scheme as grand as his, to accept greatness on the scale he'd shown them.

However, the creature he'd unleashed to do his bidding approached him with slow, unfaltering steps.

"For thirteen years, I suffered the pain of death that knew no end in order that humanity might live on."

Perhaps he wanted to worship Ben. Who could blame him? After all, was Ben not his savior?

"Thirteen years with no one to talk to, nothing to stimulate my mind, no food to eat, only pain. I watched every creature that dared draw near die, and I spent every hour thinking about the families left behind when I slaughtered those men."

Stanley reached out to his friend. "You couldn't have known—"

"Don't touch me," Busar shouted.

Wisely, old baldy backed off.

Busar's bare toes brushed the salt line. His breath, wretched with the stench of death,

"I gave up every bit of humanity I had left for the sake of saving lives, and you came here to undo that, and for what?" Busar's hands flashed out and snagged Ben's coat, twisted in the fabric, then lifted him so he was forced to balance on the tips of his toes. "I locked myself away for thirteen years, and you're just going to undo that because of some petty, childish issues you have about the fairness of life?"

Busar yanked Ben out of the salt circle and tossed him to the ground. Ben's skin burned as if the dirt and sparse weeds were lava and boiling oil. Smoke curled upward from his exposed flesh, blinding him, and overwhelming him with the scent of roasting meat. Screams so fierce they tore his throat and made him imagine he was choking on his own blood carried upward on plumes of smoke. The fabric of his clothes and the rubber of his shoes melted and fused to his skin. Desperate, he pushed to his hands and knees and reached out toward the angel who'd given him life, but the moment his eyes found her, he knew she would make no move to save him from death.

CHAPTER THIRTY-THREE

Richard

IT WASN'T THE FIRST TIME HE HAD SEEN A MONSTER BURN TO death. But even for a monster, it was a bad way to go, and the blackened, smoking remains left Richard grimacing with a sour taste in his mouth.

Loretta fell to her knees, her shining hands covering her glowing face. Glittering tears spilled from beneath her fingers. In a New York minute, Stan had her in his arms, and to Richard's horror, he started bawling too.

"He was right." Busar stared at what was left of the kid. "I cannot exist in this world without bringing death, but he was mistaken about my willpower. I can, and I will lock myself in that cage again, and you will all leave and never come back."

Good Lord, was this where Stanley learned the whole dramatic self-sacrifice bit?

"There has to be a better way." Burke came up beside Richard, Gordon following along behind her. "You don't have to live imprisoned like this. It's not right."

"The loss of lives, if I'm set free, is what's not right. I knew the risks when I chose the hunter's life. I understood from the very first day that a violent death would be the best way out."

"We have the warded cuffs we used to hold the witch's magic," Gordon said.

Busar shook his head and backed away from them. "I'd rather pace in my cage than roam the world, leashed like a dog. Besides, you have no idea if such warding would do anything against the unbalance that exists within me."

While Burke and her boyfriend argued with the dirty, naked guy, Richard pushed his dentures around with his tongue and closed his eyes. Thoughts jumped around in his mind like crickets on crack. If he could just block out the world for a second, he'd be able to latch onto the one he needed.

Loretta's sobs and the words being volleyed back and forth distracted him. The odor of Ben's remains burned his nose. Thirst lent his mouth a stale, dry taste.

Months ago, Burke urged him to learn to pay attention to his breath. At first, he'd scoffed, but he'd practiced in private and found it surprisingly effective at calming a buzzing beehive of mental activity. To a count of ten, he drew air in through his nose, felt it move down his throat into his lungs, allowed it to expand his chest and diaphragm.

Breathe in.

Breathe out.

The stale air left him, carrying away the garbage his body did not require.

"Got it!" He snatched the fluttering butterfly of thought and held on tight.

Burke, Gordon, and Busar stopped their bickering and looked at him. Stanley held Loretta in his arms, rocking her like a baby and acting like nothing else existed. Maybe, for them, nothing did. It had been like that at times with his sweet

Barbara. She sometimes shone so bright that her light eclipsed everything else. Lord, but he missed her something terrible.

Focus man!

Crap!

Had he lost the thought?

What was it?

Burke blinked and raised her eyebrows.

Oh, yeah.

"Maybe nobody else can do the thing for him," Richard said.

"Nobody can do what thing for who?" Burke asked.

"It's like a drunk or something," Richard explained.

She still didn't get it. Most times, she was just about the cleverest human he knew, but every now and then she was a little slow on the uptake.

"Busar has to fix his own problem. Loretta can't cast the spell. He's at least as strong as her when it comes to not being blown to bits by that thing. He needs to hold it in his hands and say the words himself."

Burke's head swiveled toward Busar. "Could that work?"

Busar shook his head. "If I hold that thing in my hands, I will be the most powerful creature on this planet. That's not wise."

"Letting you roam the world in your current state is not wise," Burke said. Took her a minute to catch the train, but she was riding the rails now. "You should try."

Busar tugged his long beard. "Stanley?"

Keeping his hold on Loretta, Stanley gave Busar a subtle nod.

"You are the closest thing I have to a son of my own," Busar went on. "You are the best hunter I've ever heard of. You've fought monsters I never believed were real, and you've survived it all. What say you about this?"

Stanley kissed Loretta's head and stroked her hair. "If we

give you the totem and it does not work as Richard predicts, we will all die quickly. If you don't try, we all die slowly. You told me every part of life worth living is worth a risk. If it were me, I would be frightened, but I would take the risk."

His reply must have been good enough for Busar. He strode to where the totem had fallen and lifted it with care. Magic crackled and sparked in the air like static electricity coming off dry laundry.

Busar looked at Stanley with tears in his eyes. "Thank you for coming back for me."

"I'm sorry I left. I was wrong."

"You've made your wrong right again, my friend."

The words of the spell rolled off his lips with such effortlessness that Richard couldn't help but wonder if he'd been chanting it again and again during his confinement.

Everyone braced for another explosion. An orb grew from the tip of the totem-like a fat white tomato growing on a vine. The orb shimmered, iridescent as a soap bubble. After a moment, it separated from the totem and floated in the air in front of Busar then, with a sound like sizzling bacon and a fragrance sweeter than flowers in springtime, the orb melted into the man's chest.

Trembling as if afflicted by the palsy, Busar staggered to Loretta and handed her the totem. "If you can't destroy that, take it to Heaven. Humans have no business laying hands on that kind of power."

The angel took it without comment.

Stanley rose to his feet, looking just about as unstable as the guy towering over him. They fell into one another's arms, crying like a couple of women.

Richard scanned the treetops, the disturbing valley of bones, and his scuffed-up, Velcro-closure shoes. Good Velcro sneakers weren't so easy to come by. These were starting to show signs of wear and tear. He'd have to keep an eye out for a new pair. He kicked at a pebble and watched it roll down the hill. He watched his breath plume in the air and realized that, as night approached, the temperatures were nearing the freezing point. After a moment, hoping everyone had had enough time to start pulling themselves together, he dared another peek at Stanley and Busar. They stood at arm's length, Busar, grinning, Stanley wide-eyed and shaking his head.

"No. We can stop this," Stanley said.

At first, Richard had no idea what Stan was talking about, but silver stands threaded through Busar's thick black hair and beard. Muscles faded to stringy sinew stretched over bone.

"Thirteen years without food or water. Having a complete soul has reminded my body of the reality of existing as a flesh and bone creature in a demanding world," Busar said.

"I don't want to lose you again," Stanley said. "The first time left me wandering, hopeless, for years."

Busar glanced at Richard, Burke, and Gordon, bunched up at a short distance. "You've built a new family, Stanley, and they are fine and brave, and wise. You've done well. You'll not be alone in the world." His thin legs gave out, and Stanley caught him and lowered him gently to the ground.

"There has to be a way to stop this," Stanley insisted. He implored Loretta to do something, but she just reached out with one hand and brushed Busar's hair away from his eyes.

"I've lived longer than I had a right to do." Busar's muscles contracted, pulling his skeletal body into a fetal position. "I'm tired, Stanley. Let me rest."

Possessing enough wisdom to recognize when a battle was lost, Stanley held his mentor the way he'd held his lover, like a broken child, tight against his chest. "Thank you for the life you gave me."

The rattling of a dying man's breath replaced Busar's former deep laughter. "Any other man on Earth would curse me."

Still stroking his hair, Loretta said, "Stanley is not like any other man."

So quiet and breathy were the dying man's last words, Richard might not have been able to interpret them if they hadn't been an exact echo of his own thoughts.

"That's for damn sure."

CHAPTER THIRTY-FOUR

Burke

FROM THE GLOW OF STANLEY'S FLASHLIGHT, BURKE COULD follow the progress he and Loretta made down the rocky beach. She snuggled deeper into the soft quilt, laid her head on Gordon's shoulder, and allowed the rocking motion of the porch swing to lull her into a state of calm and quiet.

Gordon, as he often did, seemed to read her mind. "Do you think your grandpa's okay?"

"He's an old man."

"He seems younger than when I first met him."

That was probably true. The man dying in a nursing home after making a lousy comeback from hip replacement surgery had been older in many ways than the hunter sleeping inside the little cabin. Still....

"I don't know how much more he can take," she said. "By the time we got back to the car, he could barely walk. One fall off the curb shattered his hip last year. How many times can he hit the ground in battle and keep getting up?"

"I don't know how many, but I suspect he's got a few battles left in him."

His warm fingers found their way under Burke's sweatshirt, and he held her with his palm pressed against her bare waist. Delicious tingles radiated from the spot, and she turned into a teenager again.

"Speaking of battle injuries, how's the shoulder?" he asked.

She shifted the joint. "Better than ever."

The light on the beach stopped moving. If memory served, Stanley and Loretta must have reached the big boulders that cut the space in uneven halves. It would be a good place to sit.

"I wonder what they're talking about?" she murmured.

"Everything. Maybe nothing. Sometimes words are just clutter."

In agreement on that, they rocked back and forth in time with the murmur of the ocean. All adrenaline from the earlier events of the evening drained away and left her spent.

She had almost dozed off when Gordon spoke again.

"You all talk about being led to the hunt. How do you know? When does that happen? What do you do in the meantime, just hang out here?"

"No, not here." She might not be certain of much, but she knew none of them would want to stay in this place, though they each had their own different reasons for feeling that way. "We're not even a whole day's drive from Seattle. I've never seen the Space Needle. When it's time to hunt, we'll know."

"Stanley resisted this hunt."

"Wouldn't you have done the same?"

Burke has known Stanley less than a year. He'd told them that before they joined him, he'd been lonely and burnt out to the point of longing for death, which implied the last year had improved over whatever happened before that. However, in ten months, the man had broken his leg, been dragged to Hell and back—literally left in the trunk of a hot car in the desert until he nearly died from heat stroke, been stabbed in the heart, died, came back, had his shadow ripped off. His darkness was restored in full measure, and now the business with Loretta and Benjamin. How did a person go on day after day like that? If she lived another hundred years, would her life resemble Stanley's?

She burrowed a little deeper into their warm nest and tried to tell herself she'd never let it come to that, and she succeeded to the degree that she drifted off to sleep, only to be woken by the flash of headlights cutting across the driveway. While they'd been gone, someone had cut away most of the wood blocking the path, leaving just enough room for a car to squeak through.

A 1969 Pontiac GTO, one shade darker than the surrounding night, rumbled up the steps and shut down. Burke jumped to her feet before she decided to stand. Gordon stood a step behind, one hand on her shoulder. She did a quick inventory. The nearest weapon was the gun in her grandfather's coat pocket, just inside the door.

The car door swung open, and one cowboy-booted foot stepped out onto the gravel, followed quickly by a second. The man who climbed out of the vehicle flashed a fangy smile at them. "You succeeded. Congratulations."

Burke sat upright. A ghoul. Had to be the ME. Every instinct in Burke's body told her to kill the monster who stood before him, but by all accounts, he was—in his way—a contributing pillar of the community. Hadn't he helped them? Hadn't he been civil when the hunters showed up on his doorstep?

"Why did you come here?" She glanced at the spot of light on the beach. Stanley and Loretta hadn't moved. No doubt they were too lost in their own melodrama to notice the arrival of the monster doc.

"May I come in?" he asked. "I'd like to talk with you."

"I appreciate that you helped us earlier, but we're not in the habit of entertaining monsters."

"Maybe you should start," he suggested. "You catch more flies with honey and all that jazz."

Gordon spoke quietly from behind her. "I think he's okay."

The ghoul gave a genteel nod of his head. "Thank you for the vote of confidence. Perhaps the lady would feel better if we spoke in the fresh air. What I have to say won't take long, but there's a problem."

"Is it about the kids?" Burke demanded. "Tell me we weren't wrong. Tell me the killing has stopped."

He laughed, showing his pointed teeth. The dim porchlight reflected in the pure black of his eyes. "Oh, it's stopped all right. No one is dying."

"That's a good thing, right?"

He held out his hands in a gesture that asked, *Who am I to say?* "It is not natural."

Burke's mind scrambled to try to understand his meaning. "Not natural for children to live long, healthy lives? I think you've confused reality with your desires."

"Your prejudice is getting the better of you," he chided.

She didn't deny it. She remained unbothered by the inclination to give this flesh-eater the benefit of the doubt.

"No one is dying, hunter. No one. People are not dying in Clallam County, nor in Seattle. In New York and Paris and Beijing, even those hanging on by the thinnest of unexplainable threads continue to hand on. *No one* is dying."

"No one, anywhere, for any reason?" Burke said.

"No one."

She'd watched Ben and Busar die right in front of her eyes. "For how long?"

"Five hours?" He shrugged. "Maybe six? It's hard to pin it down exactly."

"But word travels fast among those who eat the dead."

"Word travels fast among those whose business is facing death."

A person didn't tend to think about how many souls entered and exited the river of humanity on any given day. Burke couldn't come up with a number if pressed, but it must be in the millions. Probably thousands, maybe hundreds of thousands, each hour.

But not a single person on earth had perished in more than five hours? The ghoul was right. There was a problem.

"What could cause that to happen?" she asked.

Again, he offered his gesture of helplessness. "I'm sure I don't know, but this needs to be fixed, fast. You cannot imagine the imbalance that will result if it continues."

"Nothing good comes from imbalances," Gordon mumbled. He was learning fast.

"What do you expect us to do about it?"

The ghoul slipped his hands into the pockets of his long black coat in a gesture that reminded her of Stanley. "I don't know if you can do anything about it, but maybe you can find the guy who can."

She kept her eyes locked on his. "Who would that be?"

"Death. Last I heard, he had an apartment in Manhattan."

CHAPTER THIRTY-FIVE

Richard

Traveling eastward through light snow, Richard kept his eyes on the road and tried to control his heebie-jeebies. Some crazy stuff had happened to him on the side streets that veered off this interstate. Still, they had yet to reach Spokane, Washington. It would be at least a day before they got anywhere in the neighborhood of Spearfish Canyon. Anything could happen in a day. Why not sit back and enjoy the ride? Maybe he could talk Stan into stopping at Cracker Barrel for lunch. He had a taste for fried catfish, and theirs was as good as he'd ever had.

The wrinkled dandy sat on his side of the bench, hands folded in his lap, staring out the window, looking like a puppy that just took a hard beating. Richard swallowed his words. His friend *had* taken a beating, and it was a lot harder to bounce back from than getting knocked around with fists. In a day, Stanley had learned he had a son and watched the boy die, reunited with the closest thing he ever had to a father and watched him die, and then said goodbye to Loretta.

No matter which way you came at it, it couldn't have played out differently. The kid was wrecked. He brought on his own destruction. Busar had lived past his time. And Loretta... well.... The truth of what she told them was undeniable.

She said she had made a conscious decision to heal Burke, to involve herself in the hunt because she wanted to go home to Heaven. At some point in the past—and Richard had never quite puzzled out just when—she'd come to Earth to learn what made humans so special in the eyes of the Creator.

Man, did that comment raise some questions in Richard's mind! But before he could ask, she'd gone on. "I learned. Surely, no being of my race has ever learned more completely, but I also learned why death was given to this planet, not as a curse, but as a gift. The heart cannot take more than a lifetime. It feels too deeply, loves too profoundly. Death is a blessed release from the intensity of living. I cannot die, but I can let go of this life."

That was well and good for her, but she'd left Stanley behind, feeling all those feelings alone.

"You'll not be alone in this world," Busar had said.

Richard glanced over at the other man, the best friend he'd ever had, sitting beside him. "I'm sorry."

Stanley met his gaze and smiled. "Thank you, Richard."

"I have a question about what Loretta said, but I don't know if now's the time to be asking stuff."

Stanley smiled gently. "There's no time like the present, my friend."

Richard glanced in the rearview mirror and caught Burke watching him. He hoped he wasn't about to put his foot in his mouth and make her mad at him. "It's just that you're pretty old."

Stanley inclined his head. "That's true."

"Well, I seen with my own eyes that you can die, just like

anybody, but somehow you always come back from the brink. You're not going to just keep going on forever, are you?"

"I assure you, my friend, I am mortal and glad of it. I have no argument with anything Loretta said. I understand her decision, and someday I will follow, but not just yet. This past year has given me some rather significant reasons to hang onto life a bit longer."

"How'd you get to be this old, anyway? You never did tell us."

"It was no more than dumb luck."

Luck can come in good and bad forms, Richard mused.

A mile or so burned away beneath the tires of the Cadillac before Richard became aware of the soft clicking of Burke's nails napping against the molded plastic steering wheel. Something was bugging her.

Another mile dropped into the background.

"Something's bugging me," Burke said.

A grin tugged on the corner of Richard's mouth. "Go on, then."

"We're looking for Death, right? He's a real guy?"

"Indeed," Stanley said. "And the reason for that is interesting, given our recent conversation. Apparently, even if we chose to deliberately make the effort to leave this life right now, we couldn't do it. Death has us trapped here."

"Let's say we find him. How's that going to go? We've all cheated Death more than once."

"Not me," Gordon said. "Not in the way you all have."

Burke conceded the point, then added, "Still, is he going to be mad at us?"

"I really can't say," Stanley said.

"Have you ever heard of anything like this happening before? Do you know what might be going on?"

"I've heard of Death reaching out excessively but never failing to collect. I can't imagine what's happening."

A faded billboard sporting a painting of a dinosaur caught Richard's eye. Maybe the Grim Reaper would slaughter them all tomorrow, but today they were still breathing. And they'd be at his favorite roadside restaurant before dark. Fried catfish for lunch and, for dinner, a bacon cheeseburger, and an Old West show with dancing girls. Stan was right. Someday, it will be time to check out from this life, but today was not that day.

ALSO BY E A COMISKEY

Monsters and Mayhem

Some Monsters Never Die

Some Legends Never Die

Some Sailors Never Die

Some Loves Never Die

Some Friendships Never Die

More to Come!

To keep up on E.A. Comiskey's books and Scarsdale's other great authors, join our Newsletter.